"What if the stairway goes on forever?" she asked. "Or what if we decide we want to come back up here but this stairway doesn't exist anymore?"

He let out a breathless, exhausted laugh. "If it's come to that, it doesn't matter whether we take the stairs or not." He took her hand; reluctantly, they obeyed the lure of the yawning wall and the stairway beyond.

The stairway did not go on forever. It widened and flattened and finally ended as a ramp that eased onto the floor of a wide corridor lined with twenty-foot arched doorways. Clusters of grotesque stone faces with tiny, expressionless mouths and bulbous, hypnotic eyes adorned those arches. Beyond the archways, within ill-lit rooms, giant laborers toiled among brick ovens and over shrouded trays of quivering forms they put into and took out of those ovens. In rooms farther on, other laborers tended gigantic steaming vats in which moaning, slick-tentacled things thundered and splashed. Some of the rooms were empty, black and cold.

THE ENCYCLOPEDIA FOR BOYS

And Other Mutated Memories

by Jeffrey Osier

Contents

INTRODUCTION

For starters, I remember the circumstances I wrote all of these stories under far better than I remember the stories themselves. The ideas that triggered them, the music I was listening to when I wrote them, and of course the all-consuming emotional quagmire that was my private life – those are the memories that well up whenever I read or even think about these stories. It all seems a very long time ago now, and the Jeff who wrote these stories was a mess. But I was a hopeful mess. In fact, I'm still a hopeful mess. Just… a very different kind of hopeful mess.

Let's see, what's in this damn book, anyway?

Catalog

I wrote the first version of "Catalog" in the spring of 1978 while living in Aurora, Illinois and working as a draftsman. The less said about either of those two factettes [Factette (noun) Like a factoid, only lighter, cuter, and less relevant. Or not.], the better. I was 23 years old, a college dropout just getting ready to go back to school, and I was feeling very shaky about my prospects for the future. And then, one Saturday night, my girlfriend and I drove in to Chicago to see a midnight movie at the Three Penny Cinema on Lincoln Avenue. It was called *Eraserhead,* and I had read a review of it the previous autumn in the *Village Voice*. It had been one of those not-entirely-positive reviews that communicates a wealth of positive information in spite of itself. I knew I wanted to see the film badly, so the moment it showed up in Chicago, I was there. And, without going too deeply into *Eraserhead*, let's just say that in my shaky, depressed state, I loved the film. I also noticed that I was one of the few people in the theater who loved it, or liked it, or even didn't hate it. The imagery and soundscape of the film drew me in and stayed with me for weeks afterward. I had been writing short stories throughout that winter, and my main influences that season were Julio Cortazar and J.G. Ballard, particularly the latter's fourth novel, *Crystal World*. But *Eraserhead* blotted out all other influences that spring, and when next I sat down to write a story, it was "Catalog," a tale about a man who doesn't know who he is, and whose main occupation is collecting the little misshapen monsters who populate the swamp that surrounds a house where he lives alone, unsure if there is a world outside of his and what part he may have ever played in it. At the time, I was extremely proud of that story. Even so, it never made it out of the spiral notebook I wrote it in.

About 8½ years later, when Bill Gudmundson inquired whether I had anything to submit to his friend Mark Rainey's new magazine, "Catalog" was the story I went back to. When I reread it, I could tell immediately that it wouldn't fly. It was just a creepy surrealist pastiche. Also, it wasn't in the least bit scary. I abandoned the idea and wrote something from scratch (more about that later).

I decided to rewrite "Catalog" in the fall of 1987 because I couldn't let go of the idea. I was writing a certain kind of novella at that point: highly compressed narratives about events that span several weeks or months. I returned to the story with the idea that it was a three-act, with the original story as the basis for the third act. It appeared, like all of those early novellas, in *Deathrealm*, featuring one of my illustrations. Of all the stories that appeared in that magazine ("Catalog" was my seventh appearance in *Deathrealm*, and the magazine was only eight issues old), "Catalog" is the one that feels least like it belongs to that period of my creative life. In reality, I was building a big three-story house on the foundation of what had once been a lonely, creepy, unlovable little shack. I managed to pass it off as a big three-story house, but whenever I really stopped to think about it, it was that lonely, creepy, unlovable little shack

I was thinking of. There were worse times in my life than the spring of 1978, but few of them ever yielded up such strange and prophetic gifts.

Algae Angels

When I was in grade school, I caught little animals and kept them in jars and buckets and aquarium/terrariums. I didn't torture and kill the little beasts, but it may sometimes have seemed that way. Lightning bugs, grasshoppers, tadpoles, cricket frogs, bullheads, crayfish… Why, I once even caught a swarm of strange little swimming creatures in a mason jar only to have my father explain that these were mosquito larvae and that if they didn't die overnight, they'd be flying around our house by daylight, sucking our blood, courtesy of the convenient little holes I'd punched in the lid of the jar. It seems strange to me now that memories of this phase of my childhood asserted themselves so aggressively right after my mom died in February of 1992, and that, when writing a story dealing with her death, what I really ended up writing was a story about wriggling little creatures in those clear glass water-filled bowls that people use as hanging planters. Like many of my stories, it is filled with images from my childhood. But the plot itself, and its weird take on life after death, is all a result of me working through the death of my mom.

My cycle of horror stories was already drawing to a close when I wrote "Algae Angels," but I didn't know it yet. In fact, it wouldn't be obvious to me for several more years, though I struggled increasingly with my enthusiasm and motivation for these projects. Yet when I read "Algae Angels" now, it is obvious I wasn't writing a horror story at all. Yes, it's a fantasy about life after death, and there are patches of darkness all over it. But even with those ingredients it isn't anything that I would consider a horror story—and I'm pretty liberal in what I'll consider a horror story.

Driftglider

I remember Chicago's Big Snow of 1967 vividly. My father had just died, I appeared to be losing my mind, *but hey! Snow!* Lots and lots of snow. So in January and February of 1967, while I was beginning to manifest a number of emotional problems that would plague me for the rest of my life, I was also playing a lot in snowdrifts. I remember the first time I saw Driftglider. I knew it wasn't there. It was barely a hallucination. It was more like me imagining it was there and wishing hopelessly that it was. Twelve years later, when Chicago was hit with another epic snowstorm, I thought about Driftglider again, and I imagined many times that I saw it dancing over the tops of the snowdrifts, deft and beautiful. And of course, deadly.

What is a *driftglider*? It's a monster so fleet and graceful that even though it weighs as much as a small monkey, it can run and leap across great drifts of snow while barely leaving a mark. I did an illustration of the Driftglider, but I've always thought that it should actually look like a Dr. Seuss creation as rendered by H.R. Giger. The two main human characters, Dawn and Peter, are not based on anyone in particular, though Dawn's apartment is the second floor unit at 1751 West Albion in Chicago, in case anyone is interested. This story received some of the worst rejection comments I ever got. One of the "Driftglider" rejections was from an editor who apparently forgot to comment on the story itself and didn't start typing until he got to the part about how certain things really looked to him like signs of the downfall of... something that he was sure I was partly responsible for the downfall of. Oh well. On the other hand, it was the most popular story I ever did live readings of, possibly because, unlike most of my stories, it could be read out loud in under a half an hour.

For the Curiosity of Rats

Ah, the haunted urine story. It shouldn't come as any surprise that the inspiration for "For the Curiosity of Rats" was my first experience potty training a toddler, in this case, my daughter Rachel. I wrote a story in 1987 about "haunted urine." It felt like such a creepy idea, but the story I wrote was a piece of lifeless reportage. I never bothered submitting it anywhere. The episode ended up in an unpublished novel I labored over between 1989 and 1993. Finally, in early 1994, as my disillusionment with the whole horror-writing venture was starting to hit critical mass, I decided to have another crack at it. I got halfway through a story and suddenly realized that I was repeating the same mistakes I'd made in '87. Here I was, writing a story about a couple who'd just lost a young child, and it was as cold and lifeless as anything I'd ever written. It was only then that I realized that this story was not meant to be told in the third-person. It was meant to be a first-person confession from the person who did not believe that his dead child's urine was haunted. It was meant not to be a supernatural story at all, but rather a story about a man who goes cold on his wife's grief over their dead child because he's put off by the one ritual that keeps his wife from giving in to despair completely. Once I realized all of this, the story was easy to write. It was much harder to place, however, as I was sure it would never make it in a horror fiction anthology or magazine. I sent it to all kinds of places I would have never sent any of my horror stories to, but no one was interested. It ended up in Jon Pelan's anthology *Darkside*. It got a little notice, but it was too little too late as far as I was concerned. Notice how I talk about *every story* I wrote after 1991 as though it was my last horror story ever? That's how it felt even then.

The Encyclopedia for Boys

"The Encyclopedia for Boys" will always be one of my favorite creations in any form. It changed my life in so many ways, some good and some only temporarily good. Even now I can't read it without thinking about all of the crazy delusional things it inspired in me. I'd been writing nothing but science fiction in the early-to mid-'80s and having a terrible lack of success with it. I knew Mark Rainey peripherally through Bill Gudmundson, and I knew that Mark was hurting for good submissions for his first issue of *Deathrealm*. Only an hour or so after deciding against submitting or reworking the original "Catalog," I sat down with my fine-lined spiral notebook with absolutely no idea what to write. The first line I wrote was "Books were his life." I put it down and then paused for about thirty seconds while the rest of the page revealed itself in my head. By the time I wrote the second line, I knew what the story was about even if I didn't know where the story was going.

I had more fun writing "The Encyclopedia for Boys" than any story I wrote in that period. It was a completely amateur experience, done for love of writing and the excitement of finding out where I was taking the story, with absolutely no regard for Mark or whomever might accidentally read the story if Mark were to accidentally accept and publish it. The main influences were Borges and Bruno Schulz, specifically Borges' "The Book of Sand" and the story about the child's fascination with a mysterious book from Schulz's *Sanatorium Under the Sign of the Hourglass*, neither of which I'd read for years, but both of which were clearly on my mind. I didn't send it to Mark, I just took it to work and handed it off to Bill, who handed it off to Mark. I'm not even sure Mark liked it, but he took it anyway and so I got to see my first published story in print.

Sanctuary

Oh, there are all kinds of things I could tell you about the origins of "Sanctuary." For instance, this: in my childhood, I dreamt repeatedly about the woman being haunted by falling angelhair. Or this: while attending Southern Illinois University, I lived in a trailer for almost a year, and because of that, I had several weird apocalyptic dreams that took place in semi-abandoned trailer courts. Then there is this true anecdote: Ellen Datlow's rejection letter told me that if I could come up with a compelling *reason why all this weird stuff was happening in this story*, she'd be willing to read it again. But of course I wasn't falling for *that*.

Anyway, forget all that. Let's talk about my childhood. In fact, let's talk about the only religious experience I ever had:

Something amazing happened to Chicago television in

the fall of 1963. Horror and science fiction films that up until now had been relegated to late night television, suddenly started showing up on the afternoon movie programs that always conveniently started right about the time I got home from school. As part of ABC-affiliate Channel 7's "Big Show," which had a different movie theme for every day of the work/ school week, Mondays became their horror and science fiction day, and filled it with monster movies from American International Pictures (*Earth vs. the Spider, Amazing Colossal Man, I Was a Teenage Werewolf, Teenage Caveman, Attack of the Puppet People*, etc.). As part of CBS-affiliate Channel 2's "Early Show," Tuesdays became their horror and science fiction day, which drew from a much wider pool of films. I was just beginning the 4th Grade. Within the first month of school, my nebulous interest in all things fantastic hardened into an obsession with monster movies. Once my parents realized just how scholarly these pursuits were, I was even able to talk them into letting me watch late night horror movie programs such as Channel 5's amazing *Thrillerama*. It didn't hurt that this was also the year that *Outer Limits* premiered. By Christmas of that school year my head was swimming with dozens of monster movies and *Outer Limits* episodes.

I was reading monster magazines, watching monster movies and *Outer Limits*, making posters for horror films I thought up myself. I discovered that *TV Guide* came out nearly a week early, and that, if you bought it the day it came out, you'd know a week in advance what monster movies were going to be on TV. That in itself felt almost like science fiction. The advance notice gave me plenty of time to campaign with my parents to let me stay up until midnight or later to watch some dumb monster movie I'd absolutely die if I missed. It was because of this that I learned that Channel 7 was going to be showing a film entitled *The Day the World Ended* on a Friday night little more than a week away. The ad in *TV Guide* (yes, that's right. Channel 7 put a half page ad in *TV Guide* to announce that it was showing *The Day the World Ended* as its Friday night late movie) featured some guy (Richard Denning, as it turned out) standing in the water with a shotgun pointed at something not in the picture. Something that terrified him! What more encouragement did I need than that?

But when I woke up that Friday morning, it was to a horrible headache, sore throat, and fever. All day it wavered between 102 and 104 degrees. I could barely walk across a room I was so miserable. I only asked my mom once if I could still stay up to watch *The Day the World Ended,* but she answered me repeatedly throughout the day, every "NO" more emphatic than the last. So I ate jello and crackers and drank water and kool aid and mostly just slept the day away. My dad came home, had a highball, scarfed down dinner, and then headed out to the bowling alley, as he did every Friday night. My mom puttered around the house and I just lay sprawled across my bed, hallucinating my brains out. It was that kind of fever.

About 10 PM I got out of bed to hit the bathroom. On my way there, I passed my parents' room, where I caught a glimpse of my mom… asleep in her rocking chair. There was no sign of my dad, nor did I expect there to be any in the foreseeable future. I took a quick assessment of my condition: fever, yes, but not nearly as bad as it had been most of the day, *right?* I made a tentative detour into the living room, clicked on the TV, wandered into the kitchen, opened a Coke, poured some chips in a bowl and returned to the living room …

Of course you already know *The Day the World Ended* (1955). Just one of the period's many low-budget films depicting the woes that faced survivors of a nuclear war. In this particular tale of woe, a scientist, fearful of the horrors he'd witnessed in a nuclear test in which he'd taken part, has decided that a particular remote location (actually Bronson Canyon in Los Angeles) is the safest place to hide himself and his adult son and daughter from the effects of the imminent nuclear holocaust. The film opens with the words "The End" over a mushroom cloud. The scientist father and his daughter are worried about the son, who's missing. Meanwhile, other survivors somehow manage to wander into the valley and the modest ranch house soon becomes the last bastion of human civilization. The survivors are as follows: a small-time gangster and his ex-stripper girlfriend, a gold prospector and his mule, and a geologist who's brought along another 'survivor,' a man named Radek who is apparently dying of radiation burns and poisoning. Conflicts arise between the geologist and the gangster, who battle for genetic hegemony over the future of the human race. That is to say, over the scientist's daughter. Outside the shelter of the canyon, the radioactive atmosphere has transformed everyone and everything it hasn't killed into armored, multi-eyed mutations. Will the survivors of this little extended family ever find other survivors? Who will be killed by the mutants? And whatever happened to the missing brother?

A few scenes later, the victim of radiation poisoning, who we now realize is not dying but is transforming into a mutant himself, returns to the house late at night, telling our geologist hero that he was out hunting. Doesn't he know all the animals are contaminated? To the rest maybe, but not to him. He goes on to describe the strange world beyond the bank of clouds at the edges of the valley. He says "Wonderful things are happening out there."

I was so delirious with fever by that time that all I could think about was what those wonderful things might be. After that, nothing that happened in the film was as important as discovering what lay beyond the veil of cloud protecting the valley. Of course, a big part of the answer to that was monsters. Specifically, normal animals and humans who, through exposure to high doses of radiation, had mutated into post-atomic superbeings adapted to a life of eating other radioactive mutants and terrorizing the unmutated.

Luckily for the future of humanity, a fresh, non-radioactive rainfall was all it took to kill the monster. The film ended with our hero and heroine leaving the valley together, presumably off to help repopulate the world, while the closing title, "The Beginning," flashed thoughtfully onscreen.

By now, my fever was worse than ever, and now, on top of that, I was sick to my stomach. I turned off the TV and jumped into bed, but I was way too sick to sleep. My dad wasn't home yet and my mom was still in the rocking chair. I went back to my parents' room and shook her awake just in time to puke my guts out at her feet. So I spent the rest of the night being dumped in a cold tub when the fever hit 105, or being wrapped in blankets when I got the chills, and otherwise throwing up. And I was so confused. Things that I'd seen in the movie, or things I'd only imagined I'd seen in the movie, started getting mixed up with what was actually happening to me. Who was this big old guy hovering over me, my dad or the dad in the movie? Was I dying of radiation poisoning? Or was I not dying at all, but starting to turn into one of those armored mutations? By the time I finally got to sleep early that morning, I had no idea who I was or what world I was actually living in. And then later, once my fever had broken, I started thinking about the movie, and I swear, from that moment until I was about fourteen and saw it again, it was just about my favorite film in the world. I mean, I always knew it was just another Roger Corman cheapo monster movie and probably no better than *Attack of the Crab Monsters* or *It Conquered the World* or *Not of This Earth*.

"Wonderful things are happening out there," Radek said. I thought I knew exactly what he meant by that, even though I also grasped that what he meant by "wonderful" was something that only a mutant could understand. And I think that ultimately, I was much more interested in what was wonderful about this so-called horrible stuff than I was how scary it might be.

"Sanctuary" was the closest I ever came to making a direct response to that film and to that line. I was never able to bridge that huge gulf between the feeling of wonder it inspired in me and the feelings of dread and terror that were so much more important to the audience I was supposedly writing for.

Finally, I once had a dream about the monster from *The Day the World Ended*. I was in the house I'd lived in during high school in Naperville, IL. There was no one else in the house except for the monster, who was hidden away in my basement. Almost all I can remember about that dream was my panic and fear over the safety of the monster in the basement, and my dread of the people outside, and what they would do to the monster if they captured it, and what they would do to me for trying to protect it.

In real life, of course, I dragged the monster out of the

basement and threw him to the mob outside my door. I was silly enough to think that there might be some money and even fame in the act. But of course there wasn't. And I've been feeling guilty about that poor monster ever since.

THE ALGAE ANGELS

When I was a boy, my father would sometimes drop me off at my grandmother's apartment on Carmen Street and leave me with her for days or even weeks at a stretch. Grandma was in her mid-sixties at the time, still sharp-witted, agile, and energetic. Sometimes we'd stroll through the neighborhood, visiting her friends or browsing in the warm, cluttered shops that lined Broadway and Argyle. Sometimes we'd play tennis or take a bus downtown to visit the museums. But my favorite activities were reading and watching television in her little apartment, with its teetering displays of china, its delicate figurines, and its forest of hanging plants.

I was a sickly boy, and I'd often spend my days there subdued with fever, wrapped in blankets on her couch, Rotorooted with Kleenex and basted with Vicks Vapo-Rub. I've committed the details of my view on that couch to memory: her bookcase full of Dickens, Flaubert, Balzac, and Thackeray; her cheap, faded, nicotine-coated art prints; the folded lace curtains, worn and hanging in knots; and the glass-cased statue of the Cuirassier atop the TV.

But of course it's the hanging plants I remember most. The macramé hangers gripped fishbowls and mason jars. Within, impressive cuttings from less than impressive potted plants grew in algae-clouded water.

The algae angels lived in the green-tinted water in those hanging bowls. They were small, none more than two inches long, and lived among the tangled roots, feeding on the algae and on the guppies and brine shrimp Grandma would buy at the pet shop each weekend. When I was too sick to get up from the couch, I would stare with glazed eyes at the hanging plants by the window. I would see one or two angels swimming through the clusters of roots, lazy and graceful, far more like humans than like fish.

Their translucent skin revealed their delicate skeletons. They had a vaguely human shape, though their limbs were really long, barbed fins. An intricately twisted cord ran down the center of each limb, and the angels would untwist these cords into shimmering, hypnotic flurries of silver hair. They used their fins for swimming but used the flagella for climbing and feeding. Sometimes the angels would just hover, the flagella fanning open and shut in graceful synchronization with that of every other angel in every container in the room.

Their mouths and noses were tiny and almost human. A barbed tongue coiled in a pouch in their chests, waiting to spring out and hook guppies, or scrape against the glass to pull up algae, then slink slowly back into the transparent chest-pouch, where it resembled a jumble of intestines. Bulging atop their heads were the eyes, deep blue discs floating in red globes, pupils throbbing as they moved in and out of the root-shadows. The thick, fleshy eyelids were invisible when the eyes were open, but they were like ridged, armored crowns when they were shut.

I'd been watching them since I was too young to understand how strange and wonderful they were. I had assumed that they were something she'd picked up at the pet shop. For all I knew, everybody's Grandma kept algae angels. The first time I saw "sea monkeys" advertised in a comic book, I was sure that the cartoon of the smiling creature emerging from its egg was supposed to be an algae angel. I sent for the Sea Monkey Circus and set it up. It didn't take long to recognize the sea monkeys for what they were—the familiar brine shrimp Grandma bought by the cupful on weekends to feed to the algae angels.

"The angels are our secret, Russell," she'd tell me in hushed tones as I lay on the couch and she stood over me. The hanging bowls and their contents cast shadowy tattoos against her skin and dress. "They're ours and no one can take them away from us."

"Do they hide from other people, Grandma?"

"They don't have to, sweetheart. People never see them." She seemed proud of that fact, and she wanted me to be proud of it, too.

Sometimes I asked if I could take a few of them home but she always refused. She claimed they could never survive out of her presence. Once I even tried to steal one while she was napping. I caught the creature and dropped it into a plastic bag full of tap water. I watched it swim furiously through the clear, cold water, thrashing against the plastic wall, its blue eyes bulging in terror, looking for a way out. I knotted the bag, wrapped it in a sweatshirt and smuggled it home in my backpack, but when I finally pulled it out the water was brown and clouded with flaky white tissue. There was no other sign of the angel.

I never stole one again. Instead, I sat around her apartment, concentrating on the angels' interactions. I noticed the strange coordination of their behavior, how two on opposite sides of the room would engage in an identical dance or curl into almost perfect spheres, spinning furiously through the water and banging against the glass in perfect unison.

Throughout my ninth and tenth years I was absorbed by the tiny, green-tinted worlds of the algae angels. I would sometimes imagine that I was one of them, that I was slinking through the tangled roots, living on algae and brine shrimp and guppies, and that through the clouded green glass I was watching the inexplicable movements of giants.

When I turned eleven my father remarried. His bride, Valerie, had a stabilizing effect on him, inspiring him to insist that we—he and I and Valerie—start to behave like a family.

I balked at first, refusing to speak to her, so sure that my loyalty was to the real mother I could barely remember, but especially to my grandmother, who was the bedrock of my life. But my father was relentless in his demands and Valerie remained sweet and diplomatic through it all. Ultimately, she won me over simply because she alone could protect me from my father's anger. Over the next several years Valerie had three babies of her own—and so I went from being an only child to an eldest son. I had my tonsils out during the summer I turned twelve, and suddenly I was no longer sickly. After a pampered, withdrawn childhood, I managed to disguise myself as a fairly normal and upstanding adolescent.

Maybe my father meant to cut me off from Grandma, his ex-mother-in-law. Ore maybe it was just something that was crowded off his list of priorities. But I saw my grandmother very little after my dad's remarriage. For a while she would take the train out to the suburbs to see us or I would meet her downtown for lunch on the weekends. Eventually she began sending my Christmas cards and birthday presents by mail. I would talk to her on the telephone, but as the years went by and I had more and more distractions, I seemed to have less and less to say to her. There were moments when I'd become aware of a feeling of betrayal—to her, to the bond between us, and most of all, to that little boy who had idolized her so much. But those moments were brief and grew farther and farther apart as time passed. By the time I went off to college it had been a full year since I'd seen her, and in the next four years I talked to her on the phone only three or four times. And when we did talk, our tones were cool and detached and rarely emotional enough to even seem awkward.

She turned eighty the year I got my Master's Degree. It was impossible to imagine her so old—I still saw her in my mind's eye as she'd been fifteen years before. But I was a thousand miles away now. The old woman and the grandson she wrote to were different people from a different life. I never stopped to consider that I was her only living relative, or what it must have meant to her to maintain contact.

Somewhere along the line, my grandmother's name, address and phone number didn't survive transcription from an old to a new address book. I got married and divorced without ever mentioning that I still had one surviving grandparent. The only reason I assumed she was still alive was that I was sure that somehow my father would have heard and told me otherwise.

Was I so cold, so uncaring? In truth, I preferred to think of myself that way than to subject myself to affectionate thoughts of the old woman, which always brought on an inexplicable discomfort in me. To me she represented far more than just the insult of mortality. My bond with her seemed to represent, in a halting, repressed way, the observance of something in my nature that I could no longer bear to face.

I was living alone. What little socializing I did was in bars and theaters and other peoples' homes, so my apartment was Spartan, solitary. I drank from cartons and bottles and kept a jug of tap water in the refrigerator. It was because of that that I discovered the angels as I did—small, dead, floating transparent and nearly invisible on the water's surface. At first I dismissed it as mineral residue in the water, trapped in bits of mucus from my mouth. But then I began to notice their little dead eyeballs floating in milk and apple juice. One day I accidentally left the water jug out on the kitchen counter as I left for work. I returned home that night and found a baby algae angel swimming lazily through the water. It had been almost twenty-five years since I had seen one and nearly that long since I'd even thought about them, but suddenly the memory of the creatures flooded back into me.

I poured water into a smaller jar, fished out the angel and dropped it in, then placed the jar in the window that received the most sun. I didn't rationalize or justify my action. In a way, it was almost a reflex. Then I tracked down my grandmother with just a simple call to long distance information.

"Hello, Grandma?" I was unsure of the appropriate tone to take with a grandparent one has abandoned for over a decade. "It's me. Russell."

"Russell," she said quietly, as though unsure of who Russell might be. Her voice was deep and hoarse. When she said my name a second time it was with a strained blast of acknowledgment. "How are you, honey? Sick again?" I think the crackling sound I heard was some kind of laughter.

"No, Grandma, I'm fine. Listen…" I wasn't sure of what to say. I did everything I could to hedge around the subject of angels, but in the end, it was the reason I'd called, and I couldn't not bring them up.

She made it easy—the moment I reminded her of them, she just blurted out: "So it's starting?"

"Then you know," I replied, puzzled for a moment that she could know about it, and then chilled by the blasé sense of confirmation in her voice.

She let out a weak gurgle. "At least you were prepared, weren't you, honey?"

"No. No, I wasn't. Not at all. Grandma... what are they?" And then, feeling just a bit melodramatic, "What am I?"

No answer. I could hear her mouth clacking, could hear other sounds behind her—TV sounds, street sounds. Finally, she spoke. Her voice was clear and purposeful. "Russell, I'm not very well. Maybe you'd better come see me. Could you do that?" No reprimand. Just a simple request.

I agreed. After I hung up I sat weeping, frightened and appalled with myself. Suddenly, after all the things that had happened in my life, my memories of those fever-weakened days and weeks on my grandma's sofa had become the most significant, telling events in my life.

When I looked at my tear-dampened palms I saw streaks of thick, transparent jelly mixed in with the water, and tiny blue and white specks scattered through it. Within one of the wet folds on my right palm, something wriggled weakly. I got out my magnifying glass and examined the specks: they were tiny blue eyes.

An old woman greeted me at the front door of my grandmother's building. She glared suspiciously as I fumbled an introduction, but when I got to the part about being Betsy's grandson Russell, she perked up and motioned me in with a toothy, too-perfect-to-be-real smile. As I followed her up the stairs, the old woman—Mrs. Carroll she called herself—told me what a wonderful friend my grandma was and how spry she had been through her eighties and how it had just been in the last two years that her health had begun to deteriorate. Did I know she was 91 years old? Yes, Mrs. Carroll, I knew that.

"I don't mean to be the bearer of bad news, but I'm afraid she doesn't have long to go," she whispered just outside my grandmother's door. "You know, there's an aneurysm just under her heart, in the aorta or something, I think. It's getting bigger and weaker all the time. Poor dear refuses to let them operate, and I really can't blame her... surgery at her age. Doctor says that she'll probably feel fine up 'til the moment it bursts, and when it does, she'll go quickly. Hopefully she won't know what hit her."

I nodded quietly. Mrs. Carroll called out to Grandma, then unlocked and opened the door. "Betsy, look who's here, sweetheart. It's your grandson, Russell."

The apartment seemed incredibly small and cramped. We walked through a dark entrance way and I was ducking and bumping into hanging globes of water the whole way. There, in a wheelchair in the middle of the living room, was a tiny, fragile creature. An old, faded floral dress peeked out from under a familiar looking crazy quilt. She looked up at me. I wouldn't have had a harder time recognizing her if I'd had to identify her cleaned and bleached bones.

"Look, Betsy," Mrs. Carroll said cheerfully, "Look who it is!"

"Ambrose," my grandmother croaked.

I turned to Mrs. Carroll and she just shrugged and winked. She slipped quietly out the door.

"Ambrose, come here, boy." When the door behind me shut, it seemed as though the entire apartment—the walls, plants, the hanging globes and jars, the furniture, and especially my grandmother—seemed to let out a long, relieved exhale.

The water in the globes darkened. What had been shadows in the corner of the room began to swell and move and focus.

"I'm not Ambrose, Grandma. Ambrose is my father. I'm Russell."

"Ahh," she said, her head turning slowly, her eyes darting about the room excitedly. She started coughing and didn't stop until she regurgitated something small into her hand. She considered it momentarily, hid the hand behind her back and shook the glistening mass into a wide shallow bowl.

"Russell, then. Come and sit." Her words seemed to ricochet off the walls, as though even within all this clutter her voice could echo.

I maneuvered among her plants and sat on the couch, the same couch on which I'd spent so many days and nights in my childhood.

Shapes moved all around her, in the shadows. Dark, solid masses splashed within the hanging globes.

"Grandma, do you remember talking to me on the phone a few weeks back?" I asked, not sure she was still paying attention. "Do you remember? We were talking about something?"

"About the angels. Yes, I remember. Of course you're not Ambrose. How could that ridiculous man ever know about the angels? You're Olivia's boy. Of course." She struggled a moment. "Do you remember your mother, Russell?"

"A little. I was only six when she died."

"Your mother was so beautiful, so dainty and petite," she said, her voice slow and deliberate, the deep tones lengthening into a resonant, hypnotic drone. "Olivia was so much... so much a part of *their* world. She never paid attention to the angels, not like the rest of us did. It wasn't until you were born, I think, that she began to see them. Began to see her own. Childbirth sometimes did that to us. Brought it all on at once for your mother. Naturally, your father couldn't see them. Ambrose thought she was mad. She was. The angels... erupted out of your mother, out of every pore of her body. She didn't know how to control it or accept it. Towards the end she cried all the time, and that only made it worse. She tried killing them as they came out. She even tried killing mine. Olivia was so far gone by then that I didn't know what to do. She came here and started flinging my plants on the kitchen floor, breaking the bowls and crushing the angels. The pain was more than I could stand. They mattered more to me than anyone—even my own daughter, I decided. I just pretended I thought she was crazy, that I couldn't see any better than her husband could. We were making arrangements for her, your dad and me, when she killed herself." Grandma grew silent and for a few minutes made only occasional private clacking noises. Finally, her head drooped forward as though she'd fallen asleep.

Something leaped from the shadows and landed on the arm of her wheelchair. It was the size of a cat, but shaped more like a human. It had long, braided tentacles jutting out of its collar and sweeping down its back. Its body was a milky, translucent white, the skin mottled by lumpy clusters of purple veins riding just beneath the skin. A tiny, expressionless face hid beneath its crown of huge, deep blue eyes.

The creature pressed its fingers lightly against grandmother's forehead and tilted her head back. Then it leered at me, revealing rows of short, sharp teeth. A window clattered open and another nearly identical creature crawled in, carrying a dead, blood-soaked pigeon. The angel on my grandmother's lap leaped across the room to help its companion. Suddenly others were rising out of the shadows, hungry, eager. Eleven of them gathered on the table and window ledge and started singing a string of high-pitched, dissonant chords. One creature grabbed the curtain and pulled it open, letting in shafts of sunlight.

Overhead, the glass bowls glowed and shuddered as the tiny algae angels swam furiously among the winding roots. I began to salivate uncontrollably, feeling hundreds of tiny flagella thrash against my tongue. I swallowed the bitter birthing fluids and shuddered. I reached out to shake grandmother awake, but before my fingertips reached her I stopped. She looked so frail, so dried up and deceptively hollowed, like an exposed wasp's nest on a leafless tree in winter. She looked dead, but deep within her some vitality nestled, strong enough to prolong her life and animate her shriveling limbs.

I staggered into the kitchen. The sink was full of a foul-smelling, brownish-red liquid. A fully grown angel carrying a pigeon leg leaped past me and into the water, then turned and let out a wide-mouthed but almost silent, hissing scream, its tentacles unraveling and thrusting outward like sharp quills, before it disappeared beneath the water's surface.

Unable to control myself, I fell to my knees and vomited on grandmother's kitchen floor. The bubbling, transparent bile spread across the linoleum, dozens of pinprick blue eyes rolling through it, kicked along by their tiny flagella.

"Russell," the creature whispered in my grandmother's voice. I looked up, wiping my face on my shirt-sleeve. The creature was perched on the edge of the sink, its eyes wide and accusing as it looked from me to the puddle. "Russell," it said again, still in my grandmother's voice, "don't let them die."

I staggered back to the front room. My grandmother's head

was twisted to the side, one side of her mouth open and one eye a dark, empty slit. A line of spittle ran from the edge of her mouth, down her chin and onto the shoulder of her dress. Within that flow, things squirmed and quivered.

"It's not so bad to be a garden, Russell," the angel perched on grandmother's shoulder said. This one also spoke with her voice. "It doesn't hurt and you'll never be lonely. Your mother couldn't stand it. She didn't understand that no one outside the bloodline could see us in bloom. You live in a different world than anyone else, Russell, a crowded, more colorful world. Lovers, friends, even children will betray and leave you behind, but the angels will always be there, until the moment they let you die, and even beyond it."

As the angel spoke, it braided the lightly dancing tentacles of an angel that sat on Grandma's lap, nestled into her dress.

I thought of my mother, the tantrums, the wailing, the pool of blood. And my father, so bewildered, so ordinary; just an average man whom my mother trusted to deliver her from the madness within her cells, the elusive deformity that transformed every pore of her body into a birth canal.

The creature on Grandma's lap jumped across the room and onto a lamp table to my left. I followed as it leaped again, into the kitchen and onto the edge of the sink, next to an angel just now rising from the water. They were so near that the flesh of their arms pressed together, the milky surfaces appearing to run together into a seamless mass. Even the patterns of knotted purple veins seemed to quiver and merge the two creatures into one.

"I'm not going to sacrifice my life for you," I told them.

They answered me in my grandmother's voice, in unison. "Don't be so melodramatic, Russell. Your mother is the one who made the sacrifice. And for what? So she could live in peace with a boring, mean-spirited little man. Is that the kind of life you want?"

I told them I wanted the life I'd been striving for all my adult life. The life I wanted. The life I deserved.

For all these years I'd been thinking of Valerie as my mother. Until now, the dim memories I had of my real mother—her face, her voice, the mess she'd left behind when she killed herself— had been vague, detached, neutral. It had never occurred to me to blame anyone for what had happened. But suddenly her curse had become my curse, and it seemed that every effort I had ever made to keep myself from being alone in the world had been thwarted by the presence of these…angels, brewing to maturity within me. I was infested, and there was nothing I could do about it. I either accepted it or let it destroy me, as it had my mother.

A chorus of mournful wails rose from the living room. I found them there—dozens of them—leaping from bowls and the shadows, huddling around my grandmother. It looked as though they were suffocating her. In a panic, I grabbed the largest of the angels and pulled it off, trying to keep those teeth from making contact with my skin. When I tried to throw it across the room, it wouldn't let go of me. I lifted it over my head as it screamed my name, and then brought it down as hard as I could against the radiator, crushing it. The flesh ruptured and the creature exploded. There was little to it beyond water; just the clear, sticky skin and the weak, milky organs that fell apart as they slid down the sides of the radiator.

My grandmother screamed and leaped from the chair. Her eyes blazed with an intensity that wasn't human—wasn't even animal. The anger escaping those eyes was a celestial eruption, an unbearable concentration of light and heat suspended in a cold, lifeless blackness. The angels now hovered over her, their membranous limbs stretched into delicate winglets.

"How dare you violate me, you ungrateful little bastard!" they cried out. I wish I could say it wasn't my grandmother's voice, that somehow they had gained control of her soul, reducing her to a mindless puppet. But it was her voice—as strong and defiant as it had been when I was a child. The angels were the puppets—her satellites.

She threw herself on me like a spider, brittle limbs flailing. I tried to block the blows, push her away, but though her face was dead, her arms showed tremendous strength, less like hands and elbows and more like blades. I threw my arms up to block her and she stumbled backwards, collapsing onto her wheelchair. It was not my grandmother, but the things rippling just beneath her skin that controlled her movement. All around me, perched on bookcases and buffets and the china cabinet or watching from within the hanging water bowls, they looked at me with the shock, terror and confusion I would have expected to see on her face.

"You're a destructive fool, Russell," one croaked at me. "Just like your father. Just like one of *them*. How dare you barge in here and foul my home. My life."

I didn't know what to say or whom to direct my answers to. Grandma's mouth stretched wide and a fist-sized translucent fetus rolled out, bathed by the tears streaming down her face. It plopped, shivering and disoriented, onto the floor, scurrying into the shadows as another one emerged between her lips, and, opening its eyes for the first time, spoke to me. "Why couldn't you just leave me alone?"

The thing then leaped from her mouth, and latched onto my face, its wet, unset flesh sticking like syrup as I fell, smacking my head against the same radiator upon which I'd killed the angel.

I felt thousands of tiny feet skittering across me, thousands of glaring blue eyes, barb-tipped fins and wet, stubby hands. I heard my grandmother's voice multiplied a thousand fold, cursing me, not with hatred, but with impatience, as though scolding a small child who had just shattered a window...

I awoke slowly. When I sat up, I wasn't sure where I was or under what circumstances I had fallen asleep.

A soft white haze hung all around me. The gaps in the haze— pockets of transparent air—drifted like tiny, disembodied spirits. I heard a humming and tried to isolate it—the floating invisible beings? Or was it the squatting, wide-eyed angels? No, it seemed that the sound was a product of the haze itself, as though each molecule contributed its own tiny voice to the whole.

The three rows of glowing, translucent algae angels stretched across an immeasurable distance—an infinite regression of forms fading into the haze-glow. The nearest figures broke rank only slightly, turned inward, staring down at the lifeless husk posed tidily and modestly in the wheelchair. I peered at the body, trying to recognize my grandmother, but it could have been a knotted length of vine, draped into the shape of a wilted cross.

However, I recognized in the eyes of every one of those angels that characteristic blue-gray skepticism of my grandmother, my mother, even me. They refused to turn and acknowledge me as I rose, but I knew from the skin-stressed edges of those smiles that they knew who I was.

I wasn't hurt badly. I felt very little pain. But I knew I had made a mistake. Not an unredeemable mistake, not even the hateful mistake my mother had made. I hadn't killed Grandma; I hadn't even contributed to it. Because, of course, she wasn't really dead, though at the time I wasn't sure why I was so convinced of this.

She was alive behind the eyes of every one of the algae angels. I turned my back on them, felt the attention shift just slightly towards me, and walked out of the apartment.

Mrs. Carroll met me in the hallway, and commented on how quiet we had been all day. Had the struggle, the attack, the shattering of glass, all been part of a dream? I told her my grandmother was much worse, that I was worried and would she come take a look with me. She braced herself like someone accustomed to losing friends, with a moan, a pained expression, and a resigned nod of her head.

When we reentered the apartment it was dark, quiet and there was nothing left of Grandma except her body. That, and an apartment full of knickknacks, including dozens of hanging plants growing out of bowls of algae-clotted water. The root-tangles were motionless. Grandma looked erect, at peace, as though only fallen into an especially deep, thoughtful sleep.

I was never alone with my grandmother again.

I had already failed in my only attempt at marriage. After what I saw at Grandma's, I never again considered bringing anyone else so close to the inner core of my life.

At first I reached back to my childhood, picturing the tidy arrangement of hanging plants my grandmother had kept in her younger days. I tried to follow her example and soon discovered that, from an occasional collection of spittle into a bowl of water, several angels would develop, feeding off the algae that clung to the glass, nurturing the growth of those plants in whose roots the angels lived.

I bought an aquarium. Within two years it was a thriving community of algae angels, the largest one nearly the size of my palm. I would buy cheap, uninteresting fish, and the angels would care for, harvest and selectively devour them. I grew less and less anxious to have friends visit me, for their presence eclipsed the angels completely out of existence and cast a harsh, meaningless light on my world.

One morning I opened my eyes to find the world distorted and myself floating in cool, green-tinted water. I saw the warped, gigantic bedroom door open and a familiar figure step into the room. He looked at me in alarm...

...and I gaped at the tiny, stunned algae angel in its hanging bowl, staring at me, tiny eyes wide with disbelief.

And then I shifted back again, behind the angel's eyes. And then back to my human counterpart. And then, with only minor effort, to a number of individuals in the aquarium.

That was when it really started. I played with my soul this way, leaping from one vessel to another; first as a game, later as a challenge, and ultimately, out of an obsessive need. Eventually I could rest within several vessels at the same time. I began to see the world as the sum of an ever-increasing number of simultaneous visions.

I was able to walk freely among the people of the world, to work with deliberation and care in an office twenty miles from home. I could devote all the attention I needed to that aspect of myself while—in a way that seemed more vital and fundamental as time passed—I never really left the apartment.

I began to realize that I was not only Russell, but all the angels as well. It was only my inability to make so many mutual recognitions at once that made it seem as though I were moving from vessel to vessel.

But the Russell part of us keeps getting older. And we keep reproducing. I am able more and more to exist within a greater number of us simultaneously. But in the end, as I reach death, I'll have to reside in all of us, all at the same time, my own omniscient universe. My soul that houses a million eyes will have to merge into a single, all-seeing Eye, forever turned inward—towards the immeasurable, into that infinite regression of distinct, identical selves that will—that *must*—live on long after Russell's faded husk grows cold.

CATALOG

I

Everything was going all gray and wet. The days passed and the sky didn't clear and the rain didn't let up so much as it just varied its tone and intensity—from drizzles to downpours to fine, uniform mists. By the time the governor declared us a disaster area, we were so accustomed to the flooding and all its attendant inconveniences, we were all so numbed and unfocused by the seeping grays and the soft, insistent thunder, that there was no reason to feel shocked or proud or frightened by the statewide recognition of our situation. I remember talking to some neighbors at the train station the morning after the governor's announcement. Their reaction was just a shrug and a 'no kidding.'

It was Davey Graham's electrocution that really drove the situation home. Davey was a schoolmate of Brian's, an eight-year-old kid who died while tromping through the flood waters out near this backyard fence. Stepped on a downed live-wire, right in front of my son and five other kids.

We sobered up after that. Maggie and I stopped letting Brian leave the yard, and refused to let him out of the house during anything more than a light drizzle. That soured Brian and *that* soured Maggie, letting the gray into our house, where it began to eat away at the last remnants of color.

And of course they had it worse than I did. I worked downtown, twenty-two stories above the rain-browned pavement. The schools were all closed, so Maggie was out of a job and Brian was stuck in the house with her *as* she looked over the same assignments she'd brought home to grade the previous Friday, complaining about the *way* the school closing would cut into her vacation time and throw off the rhythm of her class. I'd come home to find them dark and listless, so I'd try to inject a little *life*, a little...color into the house. They'd just wince and turn away, and by evening's end I'd be as gloomy and numb as they were, wondering how I could have burst in only hours before, yapping like an idiot.

The weekend was a little better. We all went shopping, parking the car along the fringes of a lot that was blanketed with a sheet of water that—for all one could tell by looking at it—might have been a hundred fathoms deep. On our way home the drizzle accelerated into a torrent laced with eyeball-sized hailstones. Visibility was cut down to nothing and, for just a moment, we were reduced to a complete panic.

That gave us something to laugh about for the rest of the day. We watched the Cubs play in the Astrodome and then watched videos we'd rented at Dominick's Finer Foods and in general the mood lightened considerably.

On Sunday morning Brian put on his yellow slicker and sulked out into the back yard to play by himself. I dozed on and off in front of all the public affairs programs half-listening to Maggie's complaints about the school board, when suddenly a shaken Brian burst into the room, sprayed me with the run-off from his raincoat, and begged me to come outside with him. I was on the verge of yelling at him for 1) getting me wet, 2) waking me up, 3) disrupting my concentration, and 4) interrupting his mother, when I took a good look at his face.

Without a word, without even putting on my shoes, I followed my son out the back door onto the cold, wet grass, ignoring Maggie's questioning shouts.

He led me to the gardening shed. Our house is on the highest elevation in our neighborhood. We'd only had about an inch of flooding in our basement. Otherwise, the gardening shed at the rear of our property and the base of the slope was our only flooding problem. It was surrounded by a ring of water over a foot deep.

Brian kneeled at the edge of the water and stuck his hand

in. "Brian! Get your hand out of there!"

"Come on, dad, you gotta help me find it."

Despite the fact that I was barefoot and in a robe, in spite of the havoc this weather had been playing on my joints and in spite of the haunting image of Davey Graham, I did not lift up my son and drag him into the house. I kneeled down in the wet grass, rolled up my sleeves and stuck my arm into the cold water.

"What are we looking for, Brian?"

"Can't you feel it, dad? Swimming through the water. You gotta be fast...you...you gotta...AHH! AHHH!"

As he jumped up I feared he was going into a seizure. And then I saw the thing hanging from his hand and realized that he was convulsing with disgust and excitement. He ran, screaming, up the slope of the yard and plopped the thing onto the picnic table.

At first I thought it was the severely decomposed remains of an animal. And then I saw it breathe. Out from under the gnarled, misshapen chunk of gray flesh and thick, patchy black fur, a quivering, segmented leg appeared, raising the entire bulk as it unfolded and then stretched out straight and limp.

It was bigger than a rat, smaller than a full-grown cat, and even if broken or decomposed, could never have been either. In one sense it looked like the outer husk of an animal that had been gutted and de-boned—all loose and asymmetrical. But its three legs, all of which had three segments and a long, padded tentacle at the tip, resembled nothing I'd ever seen before.

"Dad? Can I take it in and put it in one of my specimen jars?"

"No. It's too big to fit in anything we've got. Besides, your mom'd never let you bring it in the house."

"But dad...It...it's the biggest one yet!"

And so I learned from my son how the rains had brought with them a horde of misshapen little creatures that he claimed could be found anywhere, splattering through the puddles or lying helpless or crushed on the sidewalks or encased in gelatinous beads along the surfaces of leaves. They had been trying to catch them in that flooded ditch when Davey Graham was electrocuted.

We didn't show the thing to Maggie. We tipped the picnic table and let it slide off into the grass. Brian asked for more alcohol so that he could preserve the thing. My son was already assembling a catalog of dead crayfish, frogs, grasshoppers and worms. He claimed that eventually he was going to dissect them, all part of the preparation for his career in biology. Up until now I'd found this hobby a little unsavory and was only weakly resisting Maggie's suggestion that we discourage it terminally. Suddenly the idea that the rains had brought out some kind of creature unlike any I'd ever seen before—here in a town I'd lived in for my entire life—was just too fascinating not to pursue. I figured that as long as Brian seemed so willing, there was no reason not to encourage him.

And just like that, the skies cleared. The schools reopened. With a basement full of jars and bottles and enough alcohol to preserve an entire museum exhibit, the creatures dried up and disappeared. Brian took the loss in his stride as he got back into his normal routine, but I couldn't get that one creature out of my mind. I wished that I'd let Brian bring the thing in, that thing that of course was no longer where it had fallen in the grass. I shudder now to think of the way I mourned that loss, how I lamented what I was beginning to see as the missed opportunity of a lifetime.

We had four days of clear or at least semi-clear weather after that. All over the neighborhood talk turned to flood insurance claims and the undrainable gullies at the country club.

The world seemed set back on a normal course.

Late Thursday night we were hit with high winds, a thunderstorm, and hail. On Friday morning the rain was still falling and the flood puddles so recently sucked dry were starting to refill in the yards and along the curbs. It did not let up. By Friday night, on my way home from the train station, it had escalated into a solid, roaring torrent.

I drifted in and out of sleep that night, trying to squirm out of Maggie's way as she tossed and turned all over the bed. I had to keep telling myself that it was only rain and thunder and wind. In fact, it was like nothing I'd ever heard in my life—an earth-shaking chorus, a steady and relentless wall of harmony. More than once it seemed to rise or fall in pitch so much like amplified, distorted human voices that I kept having to go to the windows just to see what could possibly be happening out there. I could see nothing except the water pounding and beading across the glass.

When morning came I was groggy and irritable. The rain had brought back all of my muscle and joint pain. I shuffled stiffly about the house, afraid to make anything more than the most timid, conservative movements.

The rain had stopped.

Maggie was in the study after breakfast, grading papers, and I was in the rec room staring at the Saturday morning cartoons when Brian came up to me with an empty jar in each hand.

"They're back, dad."

"You're sure? You've seen them?"

"*No*, but I just know they're back. It's so wet, I'm sure they are. Can I go out and hunt for some? Please?"

The truth is, I all but pushed the kid out the door. I encouraged him all the way, told him to stuff as many as he could into those two jars and I'd help him redistribute them later. I told him that if he found one too big to fit in either jar—both of which were just old peanut butter jars—to come and get me. Was that such an irresponsible thing to do, even under the circumstances? I thought there was a possibility that we'd discovered something important. I thought I was just encouraging the kid to do something he wanted to do in the first place.

I awoke with a start to the sound of Maggie, standing at the kitchen door, yelling out at Brian to come in immediately. She asked me how I could have let him go out in this kind of weather. When I tried to answer that I didn't think it was so bad I was drowned out by a burst of thunder.

"It's pouring out there and... what's he *doing* out *there!?* What's he picking up?"

I pushed past her, went out under the back awning, and put on as stern a voice as I could, telling him to come in right this instant or else, etc, etc…. He called out cheerfully that he'd be there in a second. But as I watched him through the falling rain, it began raining even harder, louder. Brian was talking to me but I couldn't understand a word he was saying. He was beginning to lose form in the deepening gray torrent of water. His yellow slicker seemed to be diffusing into space.

"Damn that boy!" Maggie pushed past me and ran into the yard shouting. I went back into the house and into the bathroom, where I dried my hair on the bath towel that was still wrapped around my head, when Maggie confronted me in a wet, raging panic.

"I can't find him! I can't find Brian!"

"What do you mean, you can't find him? Did you check down by the shed? In the garage?"

"Yes, I checked both of them. Dammit! Why did you let him go out there like that?"

"It wasn't even raining when he asked me…"

"I don't care! Go out there and get him, will you? Oh, my God! *Davey Graham*! What if…"

"Don't even think about it. Just…here, dry yourself off. I'll be right back."

I ran out the back door screaming at the top of my lungs, sounding desperate and afraid one moment, outraged and authoritative in the next, running up and down the yard and finally down to the shed, splashing through the water, searching through it with my arms and then opening the shed door. No Brian.

Running back up the slope of the yard, I tripped over something.

I reached back and picked it up. A peanut butter jar, half full of water, a half a dozen little red eyeballs spread out through a mass of folded gray flesh and patchy black hair. Holding it in my hands, not so much staring at the jar as being stared at by it, I began to hear—not the fall of rain—but the deafening, droning chorus of voices I'd heard the night before.

I dropped the jar, turned round and round, screaming my son's name at the top of my lungs, trying to catch a glimmer of that yellow slicker. I could no longer see anything at all, not even the house. I began to run, screaming out "Brian" and "Maggie," trying to detect the upward slope of my backyard, becoming completely disoriented in the process.

When I felt Maggie's hands grabbing at my shirt I had to pull her close just to see her. We were both screaming, and I doubt she could make out my words either. She pulled me up onto the porch and told me to go in and call the neighbors, or if I had to, the police, while she continued the search. I ran into the warm, dry house and just stood there, dripping in the kitchen, wondering how such a tidy and foolish place could even exist in the same world as the blinding, deafening torrent outside.

I began to wander from room to room, a trail dripping behind me. I looked at every object, not as though I'd never seen it before, but as though it no longer made sense, so close to and so shabbily protected from that watery devastation....

When I saw the telephone I had to stop and stare at it for a full minute, knowing it was somehow of immediate importance but not quite sure why. For a moment I wasn't even sure of what it was. It was only the dial tone that snapped me out of it, but was it a real dial tone? I assumed it was—it served the purpose of a dial tone. I called our three closest neighbors. Nothing. I just stood there, listening, waiting for something to happen, unable to move until that sound altered or stopped. When it stopped, I hung up the phone.

I felt nauseous and light-headed. I stumbled into the bathroom, threw up, and passed out on the tiles.

I don't know how much time passed before I got up, but in those first few moments, trying to shield my eyes from the overhead light, I had the impression that it was several hours. Maybe it was a dream I'd had while lying there, for I know that beyond that feeling of the passage of time, I was greatly disturbed about something I felt sure had happened to me while lying on that floor.

All that passed when I stepped into the kitchen and heard the roar of the falling rain.

I threw open the back door and screamed out for Maggie and Brian, but I could barely hear myself over the rain. I took several steps away from the porch with one arm stretched out behind me. The rain felt as though it was breaking through my skin, as though it was pushing me down into the spongy ground beneath me. I turned around slowly and let myself be guided back by that outstretched arm. Once again that eerie unfamiliarity struck me as I entered my own house. I tried the phone again but now it was just dead. So I paced the house, trying to run every possible scenario through my head, trying to piece together a plausible explanation for what had happened to my wife and child. Visions of Davey Graham floating in a flooded, wired ditch rose up before my eyes, but I fought them down with idyllic visions of Maggie and Brian, wrapped in blankets, drinking hot chocolate and laughing with our next door neighbors, afraid to run back over here for the same reason I was afraid to run over there and get them.

And yet, what reason was that? Was it because it was raining so hard that it was impossible to see where I was going? Of course not. I'd had the distinct impression, especially that first time, when I'd run about the yard trying to find the house, that just by being out there, I was being separated, cut off from the house…from everything.

And so I stalked my house, checking through every window, trying not to think the worst. And as I did, an image began to rise that soon overwhelmed all my other thoughts: the shimmering red eyes in the peanut butter jar, the only things that seemed to remain visible and in focus out there, visible even though the jar that held them. Even the hands that held the jar were invisible within that Wet Roaring Gray.

Eventually that gray deepened just enough to let me assume that night had fallen. By this time I'd given up trying to use the dead phone, stopped exposing my body to the pounding of the Wet Roaring Gray. I resigned myself to the fragile but more or less watertight rooms in which I'd lived for three years but never really looked at, never really *lived with*. Everywhere were signs of my wife and child, and every one of them reactivated my fear over their disappearance, which reactivated this sense of isolation, which reactivated my bewilderment over the choral droning of the Wet Roaring Gray, which brought me around again to these flimsy but sweetly furnished rooms in which I was trapped, full of signs of my wife and child, everywhere....

I fell asleep in a chair in front of the dead television. I awoke once to ask myself why the electricity worked at all. And if it did, why was the television dead? Because, I answered myself, like the telephone, like the ability to actually walk away from the house, the television was a way of connecting me with the outside. I nodded off to sleep again, hardly aware that in my perception of the situation, I had just stepped over a line.

I drifted in and out of sleep after that.

Eventually the gray outside began to lighten just a little. I got up and wandered from window to window, searching for some kind of detail beyond the rain-splattered *glass*. I wondered if the rain would go on forever, if the water level would continue to rise until it washed away the house.

I checked the basement for flooding and found three inches of water. I was surprised that there was as little water as there was, and that there was less than a half an inch of water lined up against the basement windows. Where was all that water going?

There's no point in dwelling on the droning stretch of time that followed. Outside the windows was a dark, uniform gray; the thunderous chorus hushed to a steady but almost imperceptible rumble. I didn't have the energy or inclination to step outside the door to see what was happening out there. Thoughts of Maggie and Brian drifted through my head once in a while, but I don't think I cared or even remembered what had happened to them. I would just become aware—vaguely—that they were not here with me, and then, eventually, I would forget about them again. I ate a can of fruit cocktail, pulling chunks out one at a time with my syrupy fingers. That in itself took an overwhelming amount of effort and seemed to take forever.

I continued to drift in and out of what seemed to be brief, restless sleeps, but eventually I pulled myself from the chair, tramped up the stairs, and fell asleep in my bed. I'm guessing that it was a very long sleep.

II

It was the light that woke me, the high noon sunlight of a cloudless day through unshaded windows. It would have seemed bright on any day, but after the Wet Roaring Gray it seemed unbearably hot. I lay there, trying to shield myself from it—trying to fall back asleep—until I was struck with the implications of that light, that silence. I jumped out of bed, ran downstairs and out the front door, calling their names.

The droning, listless delirium of the Wet Roaring Gray had made no impression on me. At that moment I don't think I even remembered it. It was as though I'd passed out on the bathroom floor in a rainstorm and woken up in my bed just a couple of hours later. My wife and kid were next door, out shopping, sitting in the yard, somewhere nearby, where the panic I'd felt in their absence would be snuffed out and forgotten. I ran out that door knowing exactly what I would see, having seen it so many times before, always secure in the knowledge that it would always be there.

And there it was...

My house was still on the highest elevation in the ... neighborhood. My acre and a half was still a gently sloping descent towards the outer edges of my property. But beyond those edges there were only trees. And vines. And overgrowths of grotesque weeds.

And water.

I ran all the way around my house and then stopped dead on the front porch, my eyes tearing.

I was surrounded on all sides by a vast, primeval swamp.

I ran through the house, through the garage and then back into the yard, screaming their names, trying to scream myself awake, trying to use the sheer force of my voice to shatter the monstrous illusion surrounding me. But as I did, as my mind raced and lunged after every possible explanation, my memory of the Wet Roaring Gray returned to me, that long, dream-like drone that was so obviously NOT a dream at all, during which the world as it knew it had... *what?*

Finally, I collapsed in the long, wet grass. My breathing was so strained and so laced with whimpers of horror and frustration that it took quite some time before I was able to bring it under control and *listen*.

I remained still and quiet, just waiting for a recognizable sound—cars on a road, the sound of children, distant radios or televisions, that unavoidable resonant buzz of the city only 25 miles away. I scanned the tall, unrecognizable trees. I couldn't even hear birds. Nothing. The only sound was me, shifting my weight in the grass.

I stood, brushed myself off, and made the slow descent to the edge of my property, where the ground dropped off abruptly for about a foot. Beyond that… just swamp. And slowly, as I listened, I began to hear the sounds.

At first I took them to be living sounds—the sounds of whatever creatures dwelled in those trees, in that water. But they lacked the distinct, individual voices that mark the calls and rustlings of living creatures.

What I heard instead was a soft, low rumbling that I soon realized was the sound of the swamp itself… settling. Some of these sounds seemed to originate miles away; others seemed to erupt from just beyond the first barrier of vegetation, only twenty yards away. Some seemed to actually move *through* the swamp, erupting so loudly that they shook the ground beneath my feet. Then they faded into silence.

And then, in the water directly in front of me, a slight effervescence escalated into a turbulence that seemed to define a clear and precise shape about twenty feet across. As that turbulence began to subside, a piece of solid ground began rising–a tiny islet, full of peaks and gullies and rivulets and turquoise stubs of vegetation that swelled and stretched before my eyes.

And as the water around this islet settled, I began to see small, slimy forms moving through the mud and perching on the buds of the rising, unfolding plants. I made out over a dozen of them, none of them bigger than my fist, most of them much smaller. I recognized the largest one, with its segmented, armored tentacles, the white, folded wads of flesh, the black patches of short, slime-congealed hair, the bright, translucent little nodules that looked like eyes but were scattered like a festering rash. It was just like the thing my boy... Brian, had been hunting, the thing Davey Graham had died trying to catch.

I backed away from the shoreline and up the slope of the yard, looking up at the tree lines and the clear blue sky above and then back at the house. I tried to reconstruct in my mind how the world beyond my property lines had once looked. I was struck by the overwhelming substance of the world around me, and by the gray, fading pallor of the memory of my life. Where had it all gone and why did it mean so much less to me now than it had when I'd first run out that door, less than an hour before?

I didn't leave the house for the next five days. I roamed from room to room, rummaging through Brian's toys and through Maggie's clothes, taking inventory of what little baggage we'd hauled with us from the old house three years before: our wedding album, folios of Brian's preschool drawings, my high school yearbooks. As I read through them, everything seemed to withdraw into the grain and fog in which I was supposed to see the face that had once been mine. I read all those signatures and remembered the significance of the inside jokes referred to there, but again, the very attention I paid to each little autograph seemed to distance the memory it triggered, as though in total darkness I was shining a bright light on isolated images, each of which receded the moment the light hit it. I closed the yearbook and looked out the attic window at the gigantic trees that should not have been there, knowing that the threads between these remote memories and those trees did not exist and that if they were to ever exist, it would be because my mind would have twisted itself into a shape that could accommodate both what my eyes saw and what my memory told me, all at the expense of my mind itself.

I had running water for five days. Kind of amusing, all things considered.

But as it was always quite hot in the house—even with the single window air-conditioner grinding away around the clock—I took advantage of it, bathing frequently and drinking plenty of water. I expected every turn of the faucet to be a dry, aching hiss, so that when, on the evening of that last day, the water dwindled down to a trickle, and from that petered down to nothing, I was prepared to accept it with a resigned shrug.

But the electricity held out for weeks. There was no reason why it should, of course. I mean, who was paying the bill? It would have been nice if the television had worked at least well enough to run the VCR, but it had died out during the rain, never to return. Ditto the radio. But I played discs and tapes all the time, trying to fill up that silence with meaningful sounds—sounds that had served as the soundtrack to all that jumble of memories and sensations and ideas that had been what I thought of as my inner life. But the music—especially the classical music—now seemed to shed itself of all past associations, becoming instead the living breath of the raw, blue-green turbulence surrounding my house on the hill.

I put this to the test one day, opening up all the windows, propping the speakers out of two of them and playing Ralph Vaughn-Williams' *Fantasia on a Theme of Thomas Tallis*, the piece of music I thought would clash most conspicuously with the rumbling swamp world. I stepped outside to see what would happen. The Vaughn-Williams piece, so lush and melodramatic, did not clash with my surroundings at all. In fact, it actually seemed to open up my eyes, lending its power to the mighty walls of vegetation in the distance, to the complex latticework of vines that graced the low growths near the swamp's edge, and even to the shy, slithering things that appeared only briefly, rising to the surface for a gulp of air, creeping unseen between my feet. It lent a sense of depth and importance to my surroundings that had nothing to do with the house or even me.

It was at that moment that I remembered the canoe, suspended from the ceiling of the garden shed.

My conviction had faltered a bit by the time I got the canoe down and cleaned it. I sat near the water's edge, watching the burping, crackling swamp... watching them in turn, back and forth, from the swamp to the boat, wondering what the hell I'd been thinking.

But of course I knew. For just a moment, whether because of

the music or due to that illusion of serenity beyond the water's edge, I'd seen that my only recourse was to acquaint myself with the swamp, study it, master it. I might never find the answer to what had happened to my family or to the world that seemed to have disappeared along with them. It was something that I could be separated from forever, and all the brooding and reminiscing would do nothing except break me down further. And yet, far more than the house in which I did all that brooding and reminiscing, this swamp, everything beyond the ragged edges of my property, was real, whole, and at that moment seemed to be a vast and beautiful realm in which I might be the only human being. It was mine.

My first ventures out were short and timid. I was unwilling to portage over the vegetation-choked terrain, and so I just paddled through the open water that ringed the edge of my property, occasionally moving out close to the little islets but never between them, out where there would be any vines between my house and me. The swamp was swarming with what seemed to be an overwhelming mass of primitive life, and it took me some time to persuade myself that it was safe to wander even that far.

I would circle the open waters again and again, and every time, the configuration of the landmasses and vegetation was completely different. Sometimes I would witness the rising and settling of those little morsels of land or the explosive growth of the vines and coarse grasses on the newly risen islets. But it was always the swarming creatures who commanded my attention.

At first they were little more than brown and black clouds wriggling through translucent green water. Sometimes I would see them hanging in their protective puddles of slime from the leaves and vines on a piece of land that had just emerged from the swamp. Most of them were no bigger than raindrops. They looked too frail to survive out of the water under the hot sun, all curled inside their protective gels. When I looked closer, I could *see* the rapid-fire throbbing of their hearts and the little red dots that I imagined to be their eyes.

One morning as I was walking out the door on my daily trek

into the swamp, I was confronted by a creature crawling up the front walkway. It was bigger than a cat, twisted, apparently shapeless beneath its scattered tufts of black hair. It had folds of white, pitted flesh in which tiny red eyes sat like pinlights, and legs almost identical to those of the creature Brian and I had seen on that distant rainy morning. I stood over it, taking little steps along with it as it struggled miserably up the concrete walk. I couldn't see how this thing could swim or crawl—it seemed to be in the act of dying of its own pathetic and unreasonable construction.

I shook off this grisly sight and set off in my boat for the tiny islets that wormed their way into the dark morass, where huge, scaly trees stood silent and majestic amid the turbulent rebirth and where, now, more of these fully grown monstrosities splashed about clumsily in the water, wriggling their way ashore and rolling, thrashing, and crawling through, the tangles at my feet. They were everywhere.

It was on that day that the electricity was finally... turned off. And it was also the day that, aside from a few crackers and stale cookies still snug under the sofa cushions, I ran out of food.

As the darkness soaked into me that night, I listened to the swamp and to the breezes whipping the grass surrounding my house. I thought about all those creatures out there and how hungry I would soon be, and how all that belching and gurgling out there was the voice of my new God, laying down the new law. Everything else seemed, and has seemed ever since that day, so far away.

III

While rummaging through the shambles of these upstairs rooms I found this old notebook, and so I have decided to put some things down in it—not because these things have to be said, but just because now that I hardly ever leave the upstairs I have plenty of time and nothing better to do with it.

When I first found it, I was sure that I'd written all the preceding pages myself, so I read it all with a great deal of anticipation, hoping it would shed a little light on my circumstances. But the handwriting is all wrong, and none of the things written about the wife, the child, the rain, seem at all familiar. It's true that my memory is bad and that beyond a certain point it doesn't exist at all, so I have no way of being certain that the man who wrote all the preceding pages wasn't me. But I believe that were I to be exposed to some definitive clues to my past, I would recognize them. I get nothing like that from this sad little story, as much as I try.

As I roam the house these days I have plenty of time to think about these things, wondering where I came from, why I'm here, or what has happened to my whole life.

Anyway...

I had managed to assemble, in the sealed jars that lined the downstairs walls, a wide sampling of the pathetic creatures that lived in the swamp. I don't remember my original intentions for doing so, only that I have all along had plenty of the supplies necessary for the job. There was something horrible about the sight of this catalog of life forms. Sometimes I couldn't bring myself to look at them for weeks on end, even as I continued building up the catalog day by day.

Because the doubts refused to die. Sometimes I would go out for my daily explorations and would hunger for a clue as to what the swamp had been before it was a swamp. Could I, at any given moment, be tromping or rowing over a point that had once been a street corner, a shop, a home, a tennis court? There was once a time when the words in this notebook, as false as they might ring to me now, would have filled me with all kinds of pathetic hope—hope that I was somehow connected to that man and that the idyllic suburb he'd once lived in was buried underneath the water and the restless mud and the towering fern trees.

Most of the time I identified fully with the swamp and especially with what I perceived to be my role in the ecology here. The creatures I collected for food or for the catalog seemed to offer themselves up to me. All I did was try, in my own eccentric and thoroughly unscientific manner, to erect a generation-by-generation record of the constant variation on that basic form. The house was full of jars, bottles and bowls, and I had several gallons of alcohol. Sometimes a creature I plucked out of the water would be as dry and brittle as dead leaves by the time I got home in the evening. Those, I would varnish in the basement workshop and mount atop the bookcases, mantelpiece, the dead appliances, where they would hover like twisted gargoyles. Sometimes a bottled specimen would just fall apart, leaving nothing more than an inch of floating debris atop the alcohol. I would filter out this debris and recycle the alcohol, always conscious of the fact that my task would outlast my supplies.

Every morning I would step out onto the front porch and find several creeping clumsily along the concrete. I'd pick out the fattest, most edible looking of these and, there, on the spot, tear off its pocked, hairy skin and eat the warm, bloody meat from off its cartilaginous frame.

Then I would haul the boat down to the water and set off, first taking a circuit around the house in the ring of open water and then down the most inviting channel. The dead ones would float all about me, their mouths, white cloudy films blooming out of them. Sometimes I would see a swarm of small ones tearing apart the dead, or a single large one suddenly rising to the water's surface and pulling the dead one under.

Eventually I would tie off the boat to a tree and start moving overland with my net, my club, my pack, and my plastic bags, searching for the day's most interesting specimens.

Of course I killed everything I came across. Those that aroused no interest, that resembled too strongly the basic template, I would club into bloody little puddles. That would account for about thirty or forty a day. Little ones were just something to step on in passing, way, way beyond counting.

Around midday, if I wasn't too unsettled by my morning meal, I would tear apart another one and chew off the hot meat while it was still thrashing. Otherwise I would sit back and watch the sky, waiting for a slight hint of cloud. Sometimes the land would give way beneath me and I'd be swallowed by the swamp. Once or twice I nearly drowned as I was sucked into the mire. Sometimes a growth of vines would sprout beneath me as I sat. I'd either get up and move on, or I would throw myself into a frenzied struggle, tearing away at the vines as they thrashed, pretending that I was overcoming some far more formidable attacker.

Sometimes I'd get a little lost, because even though I was adept at remembering details in the landscape around me, these same details were so misleading and unreliable that they would either be obliterated—or worse, shifted in space so as to send me off in the wrong direction. Therefore I always began to work my way back fairly early in the afternoon, at least far enough in from the tall trees so that I could see the house on the hill.

I usually returned with anywhere up to a dozen specimens a day, though no more than one ever ended up in the catalog. My choice depended on a combination of factors: resilience of the creature—because most of them were extremely delicate; how attractive—by which I mean how ingeniously hideous in appearance; and finally, how unique it would be compared to all the others in the catalog. Some were eyeless, others had anywhere from one to ten red or pink or blind-white eyes. Sometimes the eyes were even lined up in vaguely symmetrical patterns. Some had thick black manes, others were virtually hairless. A few had tooth-like or even tusk-like growths in their gaping (or sometimes meager) mouths. I tried to exercise a little taste and imagination in my choices, but down in that basement, using up the last of the daylight at the ground level windows, my arms smelling of their decomposing flesh, taste and imagination were often scarce.

Then I'd spend the rest of the evening nursing a fire and watching my catalog in the flickering light. Usually I was tired and quiet and just sat there until I fell asleep. At other times the revolting, pathetic stares of the catalog would infuriate me and I would go into a stalking, screaming rage. I'd blither hateful phrases that made no sense to me whatsoever, cursing people whose names I didn't even recognize. If I was still awake when the fire went out, I went up on the roof and stared at the star-choked sky, wondering if Earth was just an insignificant dust speck spinning around one of those lookalike stars in the deep, deep canopy above me. Sometimes I slept on the roof, other times I just sat there, listening to the gurgling and groaning of the swamp, wishing that clouds would pass between me and the rest of the universe and blot out all those painful, pointless, unanswerable questions.

How long did all this go on without any appreciable change? It's hard to say. Because of my frequent pruning and the fragility of my specimens, and mainly because I had to be conservative with my supplies, the catalog grew slowly and sometimes could shrink in half during a single day. So that was no measure. Every once in a while I'd start counting days, but I always lost track before I hit one hundred. And though my memory seems to trail only a short distance behind me, there are things I remember that seem to have come from a very remote past. I remember books and faces in picture frames lining all these walls. I don't remember what happened to them, and so I can only assume that at one time or another, they all ended up in my nightly fires.

And then it all fell apart. Listen...

I awoke one sunrise on the roof with the impression that I'd been awakened by some kind of unfamiliar noise. But as I sat up and looked around there were no sounds other than the moaning and grunting of the swamp.

I found very little waiting for me on my front steps that morning—just a few tiny, hairless creatures coasting along within their glutinous skins. I was very hungry so I ate them all, plucking them one by one up from the sidewalk and into my mouth. I was still hungry after eating all eleven of them. Hopefully, they'd nauseate me enough to dull my appetite.

There were more dead ones floating along the surface of the water than usual and almost no sign of the scavengers—large or small—that usually dined on the floating dead. I stayed out in the boat longer than usual, until a body of land erupted around me and the boat was raised out of the water entirely. I portaged until I came to a large and stable looking tree, where I tied the boat off, and then I continued overland with my collecting gear.

There was something unusual happening that day. The terrain seemed to be moving and changing more quickly and violently than usual. Signs of animal life were sparse.

I caught only one nice-sized specimen by lunchtime, and

I was so famished that I decided to eat it. I sat up on a hill, away from the water's edge and ate, watching the erratic growth around me, wondering why I was so hungry, and why this flabby, warted slab of hair and cartilage suddenly tasted so good to me. When I was done I lay on my back and actually managed to spot a few strands of cloud drifting across the sky.

I sat up with a start when I heard the first cry. There was no mistaking it: the cry of a small animal, the same sound that I was now sure had startled me awake that morning. Less than a minute later, from another point in the swamp, came another, similar sound. I stood and quietly stepped down to the water's edge, waiting for another. I had never before heard a living thing in this swamp utter a sound.

It was five minutes before I heard the next cry. This one was farther away and harder to hear. If I hadn't been waiting for it I might have missed it. But the reply, which came after only another half minute's delay, came from within the grotesque, flowered grasses just ten feet from the shoreline.

This cry was long and shrill and broken into distinct, unique fragments, like... words.

I waited until I saw an unmistakable rustling in the grass, and then stepped slowly into the water, trying to reach a possible point of intersection with whatever was cutting a line through that grass.

I saw a blur and then a splash into water only a yard to my right. I lunged, my outstretched arms thrashing through the water until my hands brushed the swimming thing. I grasped it in my hands—unsure if it was a living thing at all because of its thickness and hardness—and pulled it out of the water. And there, pinned between my hands, only inches away from my face, it screamed.

It was a head. Not a twisted mass of cartilage scrambled with ambiguous features, but a skull, a *human* skull, with gray flesh stretched over it, and two bloodshot blue eyes and an open mouth rowed with human teeth. Its neck withered into a twisted, root-like body from which three muscular, unarmored tentacles thrashed against my face. It was hairless and slimy, almost impossible to get a grip on.

But it was the expression on its face that amazed me most. It looked at me with an expression of fear and horror that must have surpassed my own, a horror so elemental and recognizable that it might have been my own face in one of my fits of delirium and disorientation, staring out at me from a mirror.

It screamed. And so I screamed, too, louder, deeper than it could. I plunged it back into the water, hoping to drown it. I felt the teeth close around my hand and I screamed again. I raised it from the water, brought it down on my cocked knee and threw it against the trunk of a tree. It bounced into the deep grass. As I struggled up onto the dry land I saw it moving through the grass, and so I leaped on it, driving its face deep into the mud, waiting for its twisted, pointed little trunk to stop thrashing.

I pinned it there until it stopped screaming, then grabbed it by the tip of its trunk and stood, staring at its mud-caked form hanging limp and lifeless. Somewhere no more than a dozen yards away, something let out a high-pitched scream of agony.

I froze and did not move until long after that sound receded into silence.

I did no more hunting or eating that day. I don't remember the trip back at all. The next thing I remember is standing at the big basement window, cleaning my specimen in a bucket of swamp water.

Its eyes and mouth were closed now, its face peaceful and composed, but I could not forget the look on its face as it struggled. The disquieting novelty of so familiar a set of human features suddenly appearing within the zoological stew of the swamp had a strange effect on me. Perhaps I was in shock. I was in a subdued, listless state for a number of hours. Then, I roused myself, threw out three perfectly good specimens, and used the biggest jar I could find to set up this new creature in the catalog. It was a natural if incongruent centerpiece. I sat in the big chair, sometimes staring at the dead television, sometimes staring at the catalog. After I lit my little fires I searched through the room for anything that might have a photograph or even a drawing of another human face. There was nothing. Maybe upstairs, in the attic. I doubted it. It occurred to me that mine was the only human head, or even image of a human head, in the entire house filled with the grotesque, shapeless little non-faces of my catalog.

Until now.

I fell asleep on the chair as the embers dimmed in their bowls. I don't know how long a sleep it was, only that it was cut short by a sound. A scream.

I leaped out of the chair shouting a word. By the time I reached the jar I no longer remembered the word, only the force with which it had erupted into my head and out of my mouth. I lit a small fire and held it up to the jar.

The eyes were wide open. The mouth was slightly open as well, with just a little bit of tongue protruding between its even rows of teeth. It was bobbing slightly in the alcohol, its shriveled, pointed trunk curled inward towards the face, the tentacles twisted and twined together as though in prayer.

I stared at it in the flamelight, trying to remember the word.

I did not go out for several days after that. I finished searching the house for human faces, but there were none. I tried to avoid looking at the catalog and especially that biggest jar, but it was impossible. No matter what I tried to focus on, no matter where I hid, I always ended up there, before the floating face.

The mouth and eyes were shut. It did not move.

When I finally went out it was without any hunting gear. I stayed in or at least close to the boat the whole day. I saw the usual number of creatures and except in the usual way, they were all just as alike as they'd ever been. I didn't try to catch them or kill them. All I did, really, was listen.

I was waiting for another cry another *voice.* But there was nothing. Not even…

A chill ran through me when I realized it late that afternoon. I had been straining my ears so much for that special sound that I hadn't even noticed that the swamp itself had… settled. No more epic rises or falls in the terrain. No turbulence in the water. I tried to recall a single incident that day in which the ground or the plants had moved.

When the significance of this silence struck me, something else occurred to me as well. I was being watched in silent judgment.

It was already getting dark when I dragged the boat through the long yellow grass and into the shed. I thought of the desolate darkness of that house and wondered which was worse, being in there with that dead face, or out here with that quiet yet immense presence. I walked around and around the outside of the house, watching the sky darken, watching all those stars blink on for the night and then went down to the water's edge.

It seemed to me that even at that moment, the silence intensified. In expectation.

"All right!" I screamed. "Here I am!"

Just silence, swallowing up my voice. The distant trees were like the pointed caps of judges, even blacker than the night.

"I-I'm sorry. I didn't mean to kill it!" I burst into tears.

"I realize he's...he's... what? Who was he? Tell me!"

Time passed. The stars were coming out now, waiting to hear what I'd say next.

"Listen. I'll stop. I haven't eaten in days, but... I'll stop. I'll eat weeds. Just... talk to me. Please. Don't go away now."

A sound. A voice. Just a voice, very far away.

It was answered by another, this one not so far away. A third voice joined in... and then another. It then quickly swelled into a chorus, as hundreds, then thousands of voices spoke a single, one syllable chant, over and over again. I stood. I looked into the sky. The deafening sound, so familiar somehow, seemed to be crashing down from the sky, and for a moment I winced at the thought that tons of water were about to come crashing down upon me.

As I hurried up the hill I realized that they were all around me now, all saying the same word, all with this long, maddening melodic monotony. I threw open the door and locked myself into the foul darkness of the house. The walls didn't close off the sound enough. I wondered how this feeble, fragile structure could withstand the thousands of chanting creatures in the grass and the swamp. . .in the sky.

"Bill...Bill..."

The voice was near my head, on the stairway.

And now, hundreds of voices erupted in the darkened rooms around me, all saying..."Bill...Bill..."

A jar struck my head. Alcohol splashed over me and a wriggling monster slapped against my leg, sending me crashing onto the broken glass. All my screaming could not drown out that word.

They leaped on me, skittered over me, perched atop me, all jabbering, madly. For a moment I was sure they were going to completely envelop me, tear me apart and devour me with all those teeth. I dragged myself through the darkness and finally got to my feet. My left knee, which had hit hard when I'd gone down, was throbbing. I couldn't bend it as I climbed the stairway.

By the time I made it to the top I had shaken them all free.

They didn't seem to have any interest in following me. I could hear glass breaking, I could hear the fever pitch of their chattering and every once in a while, amid all those unfamiliar sounds, that single word reached out across the gulf and slapped me. *Bill.*

I slept on the roof that night. And every night since. How many nights that adds up to, I don't know. I haven't eaten or taken a drink of water, so I suppose it can't have been *that* long. And yet, how could it not be?

I just closed this notebook and opened it again. The name on the upper right of the cover is William Parkinson. What *that* means, I don't know. I can only depend on my memory and my perception of the world around me. It would seem likely that, despite my memory, or lack of it, and despite the difference, slight as it may be, in the handwriting, that I am, or once was, that pathetic young family man. It's still a little bright out. Maybe I'll reread all of that stuff now. Maybe I'll feel differently about it than I did when I found it this morning while rummaging through the clutter in the attic.

Otherwise, I have nothing else to say…

Morning. A strange, gray morning, following the first starless night in my memory. I feel weak and it's getting hard to swallow.

The level of the swamp has been sinking. It's receded back into the weeds and the motionless vines. Once I noticed a change in the skyline, as though the horizon was more diffused, farther away. Now I realize that the tall, pointed trees that fenced out those great distances are all disappearing. This morning I actually saw one fall. I heard it crash.

Of course that first night on the roof was very loud and chaotic. They were very quiet the next day, and except for the turbulent paths they cut through the long grasses, I saw no trace of them. Occasionally I would hear them downstairs, talking or shuffling through the broken glass. For the last three days, I haven't even heard that.

But things are happening out there. I am getting very thirsty and will eventually have to go outside and get some water. I can no longer even see the water, but of course it's there. Just a longer walk, out past the edges of the long grass and onto that smooth gray expanse that separates it from the tangles of the drying swamp.

I had always considered the swamp so wholly mine, as a vast extension of the blood coursing through me. The realization that it was something apart from me, perhaps antagonistic to me, was a humbling blow. But now I can see that, of course, that's the way it has always been, whether I realized it or not. And I survived. And so I shall survive. I'll go downstairs and out that door and down to the water's edge, wherever that might be.

But I am puzzled. I can no longer visualize the catalog. What the twisted little specimens in the jars looked like. What the… face looked like. Or, for that matter, what my own face looks like. Everything seems to be receding, like the stars, the water's edge.

Changing… Last night, through the fog, I saw lights. Flashes and rumbles filled the sky for brief instants. Lights that glowed within the trees and tangles of the swamp, and some that even cut trails through the fog. Am I going back? Am I going to an even farther, more desolate and lonely extreme? And what of my own will I take with me? If I burn this notebook, will I pass through these changes with nothing at all?

Another tree has just fallen. In the distance, I seem to see a tall, smooth, reflective structure. It comes and goes through the fog.

Oh, god, I need a….

Funny. I was about to write *drink of water* when a drop of the stuff splattered on the exact spot where I was going to write it. *Water* is falling out of the sky. Rain.

I'm inside now. I heard a horrible screeching in the bathroom up here and went in to find that a foul, viscous substance is dripping slowly from the faucets, accompanied by the awakening squeals of the long dormant pipes. It's a maddening sound but if I stay close to the windows it isn't so bad. It's drowned out by the sound of falling water, as the whole world returns to the Wet Roaring Gray.

DRIFTGLIDER

Dawn sat at the window for half the night, an occasional fingertip brushing over the swelling on her upper lip as she watched the snowflakes drifting in illuminated diagonals outside her living room windows. She envisioned Peter's car sliding off the road and into a tree, or better yet, over the snow-covered yellow line and into the path of a tractor-trailer. She'd gone through drawer after drawer until coming up with that last pack of cigarettes she'd hidden a year and a half ago, just so she could sit at the window and smoke herself nauseous, dreaming of her lover's violent death.

When she awoke in the morning, there was a foot and a half of snow on the ground. The swelling over the center of her lip was big and purple and bisected by a fresh, brittle scab. She'd never get away without having to explain that to somebody at work. In the meantime, her empty stomach churned, her head ached and her back tensed at the mere thought of having to dig her car out of the snow.

She took the landlord's snow shovel from its hook on the basement stairs and hauled it out to her car—along with a half-empty bag of salt. It was six A.M. on a Monday morning and the entire block, a stretch of tightly packed three-flats on both sides of a quiet, residential street, was deserted and silent. The cold was bitter and the wind blew the upper layers of the snowdrifts in stinging arabesques.

Dawn's muscles ached from her brief struggle with Peter the night before. Her back and shoulders erupted with pain every time she lifted the shovel. She tried to ignore it, tried to stop superimposing his arrogant sneer onto the untrodden sheets of new snow. She tried not to hear the calm, cruel hiss of his voice tainting every howl of the wind. But it was impossible. In a way that only her pain and discomfort could justify, the cold and the snow that threatened to immobilize her were an extension of the grip Peter had on her: brutal and indifferent, something that had to be surmountable but nevertheless appeared limitless, something that could spill over at any moment and suffocate her without any fear of retribution.

When she finished brushing off the car and clearing a path out of her parking space, she stopped to gaze at the blanket of snow around her. The snow transformed the entire block: swelling on rooftops, marbling the brick, and clustering in such unbroken sheets upon the tree branches that there seemed to be no difference between the trees and the snowdrifts that angled towards them. Her Plymouth Sundance was the only uncovered car. Even though two sets of tire tracks cut a path through the eighteen inches of snow, it seemed as though she and her car had been transported to a desolate alien landscape. The faint resemblance it bore to her home was just a cruel trick her mind was playing on her.

Why isn't anyone else out here? Could the office be closed today? Should I be listening to the radio? It sounded too good to be true. And even if it were, she had to try to get downtown, or at least to the nearest L station. There was no way she could stay in that apartment all day, unable to go anywhere. The walls still echoed with Peter's quiet, deadly threats. The stink of his bloodlust was so pervasive that it had followed her even out here.

Halfway down the block, she saw a small, dark figure moving swiftly across the snow. She spread salt across the path that would lead her into the middle of the street and then took the salt bag and the shovel back to the basement stairs. When she returned to her car she saw an old man at the near end of the block, sweeping the snow off the roof of his Buick. As she opened the door to get into her car, she saw the small figure again, gliding over the sheer white landscape like a wild animal racing across a glacier. It was not a child. It seemed to move with the four-legged gait of a monkey, but it wasn't a monkey, either. An array of crests or feathers crowned its head and ran down its back, waving gracefully in time to the creature's movements. She saw it race up a snowdrift that the wind had sculpted to a particularly vertical angle. When it reached the lip of the drift, it leaped into space and she lost sight of it. She slammed her car door and stood in the street, staring at the spot at which she'd last seen it. Had it just disappeared into thin air? She walked across the street to examine the snowdrift and found that the footsteps she'd seen the animal make had left no impression whatsoever on the snow that had fallen only hours before and which was still as loose as powder. As she ran her ungloved palm over the surface, she tried to picture the creature she thought she'd seen. Had she imagined it? She leaned towards the delicate lip of the snowdrift. There, in precisely the spot where she had seen the creature take its great leap into space, was an impression in the snow—the shallow print of a tiny footpad and three long claws.

It was the worst Chicago winter in over a decade—one blizzard after another, while temperatures on those rare days between blizzards never rose above freezing. Snowplows, cars, trudging adults, and tireless children desecrated and rearranged the snow, packing it tight and slick and piling it into hills that grew darker and dirtier—but only until the new snow fell and erased all traces of human intervention. It was all anyone seemed to talk about, and had it been an election year there was no doubt that the sheer logistical impossibility of keeping the streets clear and safe would have cost yet another mayor a job.

Dawn had problems of her own to contend with, and she never bothered to complain about the snow or even listen when others did. It seemed that no obstruction in the world—good or bad—could keep Peter away from her. She spent all her waking hours torn between two thoughts: the fear that Peter would kill her, and the fantasy that Peter himself would somehow die and cease to terrorize her.

And yet, sometimes she would stop and wonder why it was so difficult to remove him from her life. What was so different about Peter? Was it the fact that she knew so little about him, other than he was either married or living with another woman and that he was, above and beyond anything else, a hunter?

Was it that Peter had such a knack for making her feel taken care of? He would cook for her, shop for her, do handiwork around the apartment, and massage her knotted muscles. Dawn had spent so many years taking care of other people: her parents, her younger brother and sister, most of her friends in one way or another, and nearly every hopeless man she'd ever been involved with. She'd long since reached the point where she felt she was one of the few self-reliant people she'd ever really known, and this was a considerable source of pride. And without overtly denying or dismissing this quality, Peter, a blonde and ruddy stranger with a crooked smile, stepped up to her at a party and gently took it all away.

If Peter called and asked to come over and make her Shrimp Vesuvio, it wasn't his threatening presence she would be thinking of, it would be the incomparable taste and aroma of his cooking. If he came over unannounced, he always managed to get past the locked lobby door, up to the second floor to her apartment, where he would just say, in a light purring voice, "Open the door, Dawn." And it wasn't exactly fear of retribution that made her finally open it. It wasn't guilt and it wasn't embarrassment. Dawn couldn't figure out what it was, and meanwhile, every time she acquiesced to his desire to see her for a few more hours, she was almost surely putting herself in line for a vicious pinch or squeeze or slap or punch or kick or choke. Peter never spoke a rude or unkind word; he merely exacted a certain amount of pain as payment for his good will.

On the first of two occasions he'd stayed the entire night with her, he'd brought a handgun, a .22 to hide under his pillow, saying that it was the only way he could keep from having nightmares. On the second night he not only brought the gun but left it there, as if to say, "See? Now you know I'll always be back." Or maybe, "Try to kill me? Well, here's your chance."

Shoveling her car out of the snow became the therapeutic focal point of her life. She actually began to look forward to the deep snows that would force her outside before sunup to dig out the car, even on weekends when she had nowhere to go. And just as Peter always obliged her worst nightmares, the weather always obliged her most pointless, repetitive labors.

Driftglider was always there. The creature appeared with every new snowfall. She'd long since dismissed the idea that it was a figment of her imagination. She would see Driftglider from her windows late in the evening, and on the mornings when she had to dig her way out, it would be dancing as though weightless upon the drifts and roofs of abandoned cars. At first she wasn't sure it noticed her. Yet, how could it not, when she was almost always the only one out so early? Soon, she realized that it not only knew she was there, but it was performing *for* her. Slowly, it was building the courage to draw closer. She began to hear its call: a light, airy coo.

Sometimes at night she would dream that she was following Driftglider through the snow. It would halt at the peak of a shimmering glacier and turn to her with a beautiful, soulful face and smile before continuing on its way. In her dreams it was never cold. She could move over the snow with the same weightless grace as Driftglider, and she knew that once it let her catch up, they would have arrived at someplace wonderful. When she awoke from one of these dreams, her hand was clutching Peter's gun, which she now kept under her pillow at all times. The barrel was pushing into her palm.

On the morning the city finally gave up and shut down, she sat in the apartment listening to the radio. Between songs the deejay would run down the list of schools and corporate offices closed for the day (it would have probably been quicker to name the ones that had stayed open), give the latest temperature (minus 23 degrees at O'Hare, minus 16 at the lake, with a wind chill of forty-two degrees below zero), and a reminder that when it had finally stopped falling the night before, there had been an accumulation of five inches of new snow. Dawn sat with glazed eyes, looking out the window at the white wasteland and daydreaming of icicles—which seemed like an almost tropical impossibility at this point—and worrying about the phone ringing. Every time she heard a noise in the hallway—usually Mr. or Mrs. Colouris, or Mrs. Winston, the old woman upstairs—she was afraid it would turn out to be Peter, that he would knock on her door and say, in his silky baritone,

"Open the door, Dawn." Once the phone rang and she refused to answer. It rang twenty-three times before the caller gave up.

Finally she couldn't stand it anymore. She wasn't going anywhere, and even if she wanted to, there was no way her car would start. But she had to get out of the apartment, had to get away from the thought that Peter would show up, had to get the car out from under all that snow.

Had to see Driftglider.

"Dawn, you shouldn't be goin' out there!" Mr. Colouris called from the basement when he saw her grab the shovel from the stairway. "You stay inside where it's warm! You got the rest of your—" The door slammed on his words of wisdom.

She needn't have brought the shovel. The car was clear of snow and a path cleared out into the street for it. On the roof of the car sat Driftglider, squatting like a gargoyle, fidgeting like a monkey, displaying its razor-edged plumage like some nightmare bird-of-prey. It looked at her with soulful eyes as she stepped up to the car, eyes that were large and brown and wet like glistening, gravity-defying pools. There was nevertheless something very human about that face. Or maybe there was just something human about her attraction to it. Its plumage was like nothing she had ever seen, a marble-swirl of deep earth tones, each stalk lined with bristles that seemed alternately feathery and thorny. Somewhere behind her a door slammed. Driftglider gave a very human look of terror over her shoulder, then leaped from the roof of the car and disappeared in the snow.

When Dawn turned she saw the little old man from next door with his dog. The man kept his eyes to the ground, anxious for the dog to relieve itself so they could both get the hell into the house. He didn't seem to notice Driftglider. Dawn went back inside, calm and detached. For the rest of the day she could think of only one thing: Driftglider's face, more beautiful than in any dream.

Two nights later, after a particularly ugly evening with Peter, another blizzard swept over the city. The windows rattled and whistled, but Dawn still managed to drift in and out of sleep enough to keep her in bed until the phone rang at five-thirty in the morning.

"Dawn. It's Peter. Have you looked out your window yet?"

"Peter, what do you want?"

"Are you driving to work today?"

"I suppose I am. Why?"

"Because we just got another four inches of snow. Let me give you a ride."

"I don't want you to give me a ride."

"Dawn." There was a quiet, malicious patience in his voice. "Now don't get mad about last night. You know what I've said about you getting mad like that."

"If you come over here, I'm calling the police."

"And telling them what? That you don't want me to dig out your car? Dawn, Dawn, you aren't going to call them. You can't and you won't."

"Bastard!" she screamed as she hung up.

She was dressed and out in the street in less than five minutes. There was Driftglider, perched atop her unburied car, waiting for her. The moment she set eyes on it all the cluttered sounds and thoughts and intrusions seemed to fade out of existence. If there were brick walls and windows hidden beneath the rolling contours of snow, they and the people that dwelled within them could touch neither her nor Driftglider. She knew she was awake, knew that it had been Peter's voice on the phone and that yes, this was just another Thursday, just another workday, but as she stepped up to Driftglider and locked eyes with it, she felt protected by the cumulative strength her dreams had built up within her.

She removed her right glove and held her hand out. Driftglider pressed its fingers forward, into her grasp, its skin hard and thorny; yet the touch was light—gentle and thoughtful. It looked down at their merging fingers and then up at her, blinking its deep, reflective eye pools and tilting its head as it cooed, as though it were talking to her.

"I wish there was something I could do about you," she whispered. "Something I could do for us." She smiled at it, trying to reinforce the comforting assurance in her voice.

It responded by extending a long, lumpy and thorn-ridged tongue from its narrow, nearly invisible mouth, and using it to scratch at the ridges above its eyes.

She did not hear the truck pull up alongside, only heard Peter shift it into neutral. When she looked up he was climbing out of the open door, eyes and mouth wide, staring at Driftglider with an expression that was unequal parts fear and amazement.

Dawn pushed Driftglider, cutting her ungloved palm on the thorns of its bony arms. "Run!" she cried, "Get out of here! Quick!' It leaped from the roof of her car to the roof of the next, and then disappeared between two others.

When Peter ran up there was a rifle in his hand.

"Dawn! What was that?"

"What are you doing with that? What do you need a gun for?"

"Answer my question," he hissed, grabbing her wrist and pulling it up between their faces, squeezing. "What was that animal?"

"A dog, just one of the neighbor's dogs. I was shooing it off the car. You can't go around killing peoples' dogs."

Without hardening the expression on his face—at times like this his face was at its gentlest—he slapped her. She grabbed the rifle but he shoved her away and struck her in the stomach with the rifle butt, knocking her to the ground. Dawn collapsed in the snow as Peter ran from car to car, pausing with rifle poised between each one, trying to catch sight of Driftglider.

"Bastard," she hissed, clenching her fist as she stood. "I *am* calling the police!" she shouted.

She ran into the building and up the stairs, her face hot with embarrassment and rage. *So now he's taken it into the open where everybody can see it. That's fine. See if he can keep me his little secret now!*

She sat on her bed and lifted the receiver, then slammed it down again. She turned and reached under the pillow. Peter's .22 was still there. She lifted it and tried to imagine herself firing it. *I'll just walk up to him, and when I get close enough I'll just….*

What?

She eased the gun into her coat pocket, went downstairs and out the door into the snow again, remembering that the last time she'd seen Peter he was carrying a rifle. *So now we're going to have a shootout in the street. There must be at least 200 people living on this block and every time I turn around, it seems more like my own private, bleach-white fantasy world.*

She couldn't see Peter anywhere, but his truck was still idling in the middle of the street. Near her car was a pile of snow four feet high, built up from weeks of her own shovel-loads now that she was able to get the same parking spot literally every day. Perched atop the snow pile was Driftglider, staring into space, paying no attention to her. As she stepped towards it she saw the slashes and pools of blood seeping into the snow, saw the pink, lumpy sinews extending from Driftglider's clenched jaws down into the bloody mass half-buried in the snow pile, the bloody mass blossoming from the rip in Peter's leather coat.

Dawn did not scream. She took the gun out of her pocket and held it to Driftglider's head. It glanced briefly at the gun and then gave her a glazed, lazy glance before returning its attention to the red, steaming meal nestled in the snow beneath it. She put the gun away, lifted the rifle from the snow and hopped into Peter's truck. Dawn had no idea where Peter lived, who to contact even if she wanted to tell anyone what had happened to him. She sat behind the wheel, toying with the keys and wondering if anyone anywhere knew about her and Peter, if there was anything in the world to connect them. She drove the truck down to the Fullerton L station, parked it, and took the train back home, trudging the mile and a half from the station. When she reached her car, she found that Peter's corpse was no longer visible on the snow pile. Had Driftglider eaten it all? There were signs of a struggle, but no blood. She thought she could see something within the snow pile, but could it actually be Peter? Or were her eyes just playing tricks?

She went inside and for the first time in seven years, called in sick and went back to bed. In her dreams the snow had all melted and the rapidly decomposing corpses of all the humans and animals that had died and been buried within the drifts were hissing and shimmering, exposed beneath a hot, stern-faced sun.

By mid-March the snowfalls had dwindled to no more than an

occasional flurry. Every once in a while the temperature would creep into the forties and fifties, and eventually little splotches of black and green began to peek through the dirtied snow. Dawn tread carefully no matter where she went or what she did. She had her own reasons for being afraid of what the melted snow might reveal. She put in as many hours at the office as she could, but now she left more and more of her work with her secretary, unable to keep her attention from wandering into the gray, diffuse haze that seemed to be swallowing her. Every time the telephone rang she feared it was someone calling to ask about Peter, so she let her answering machine screen every call. But no one ever called about him. There were times when she couldn't believe that their association, all-consuming and deadly as it had been, could have really been so tenuous, so secretive; there were other times when she wondered if there had ever been a Peter at all.

Or if there had ever been a Driftglider.

Something was buried in that snow pile. It was the most tenacious bank of snow on the block, blackening and hardening and still almost three feet high while the snow almost everywhere else was completely melted away. Dawn could see the configurations of the thing buried there—Peter's half-eaten corpse—riding just beneath its surface, as though all it would take was one more fifty-degree day for it to blossom, the first rotting flower of spring.

She worked late one night and, for the first time in months, had to park her car on the next block. Walking towards her apartment, she heard a high-pitched, frail moaning coming from a row of hedges along the corner three-flat. She stopped and saw a silhouetted shape emerge from the leafless shrubberies. There was no mistaking the adornments that crowned its back, even though they were bent and drooping. *Driftglider.* She called it by the name she had given it in her dreams as it stumbled towards her, still moaning, a foul odor preceding it. Driftglider was dying. Trapped here with nowhere else to go, the thaw was killing it.

She knelt before it, cupping her palm against its cheek—wet and fleshy, no longer brittle and slick—and raised its face towards her.

It was not Driftglider's face. Stretched across its thorn-framed head, atop its thin, nearly weightless body, was Peter's face.

She jumped back with a yelp. Its mouth stretched wide, contorting Peter's face into a visage of unimaginable pain. It let out a scream that set off every dog in the neighborhood.

As she hurried down the block and pushed open the door to her building, she could no longer hear Driftglider, only the dogs.

Four days later, she took a spade from Colouris' tool rack on the basement stairs and hacked the stubborn snow pile down to its base. All she found in it were a few rags dangling off a rusted length of zipper. There was no way to be positive, but Dawn was sure it was Peter's jacket. She threw the rags away, replaced the spade on the basement stairs and then went back to her apartment, where she sat for the rest of the afternoon, fondling the gun Peter had left behind, her only proof that the man had ever existed.

It was raining on the Sunday morning she finally found Driftglider. It was no more than a few limp strands of tissue, only an insubstantial echo of its once beautiful form, its head buried in the mud. She glanced at it, passed it by, and was already to her car when she turned and ran back to it, pulling it out of the mud by the strand that had once been its torso. It seemed to almost come apart in her hands as the outer layers smeared and dripped. The moment she lifted it out of the mud it began to cry.

Dawn ran, dragging it along behind her, frantic, unsure of what she could do for it, where she would put it, only sure that this magnificent beast could not just rot away in the mud, food for the worms and ants.

She threw open the door and began running up the stairs when Mrs. Colouris opened her apartment door. The woman took one look at the thing Dawn was dragging along behind her and screamed; Dawn ignored her and kept going. She could feel the weight growing lighter, as though each step the body bounced against gouged away a little bit more. She heard Mr. Colouris below, pushing his wife aside and shouting up at Dawn.

"You crazy bitch! Jesus Christ! You crazy bitch! I'm calling the cops."

Mrs. Winston from the third floor was on her way down as

Dawn fumbled for her keys. The old woman looked at the thing dangling from Dawn's arms and covered her mouth, groaning in revulsion as she retreated up the stairs.

Even after she slammed the door Dawn could still hear Mrs. Colouris screaming and Mr. Colouris shouting out threats. Sometime in the unimaginably distant future, she would have to deal with them, but so much had to happen before then….

Driftglider was coming apart in her arms, yet it still had breath, still had warmth and life. *Where can I put it? What would bring it back, revive it? The cold!*

She threw open her freezer and scooped out its contents with a wave of her forearm, then threw in the still-moaning pieces of flesh. She shut the freezer door and the moaning stopped. She listened carefully, but could no longer hear screaming or yelling from downstairs.

Dawn collapsed on a living room chair, pulled the gun out from under the cushion and looked at it with dazed and unfocused curiosity.

She didn't see the flashing red lights outside the window until she heard the banging at the door. She sat up with a start, replaced the gun beneath the chair cushion and crept to the door.

They called out to her. Mr. Colouris was there, but she was sure he was not doing the knocking, and he surely wasn't the one asking her to please open the door. Dawn put her hand on the doorknob, then pulled it away.

She went to the kitchen and opened the freezer door. Cold, moist air billowed out of the opening. Something in there was coughing and gasping for breath. Scattered across a layer of freezer frost were strands of decomposing tissue that even now she could recognize for what they had once been. A part of a leg, the crumpled stump of a once majestic crest, all of it converging on a throbbing lump in the center of the freezer. And perched upon it, growing out of that lump, Peter's death-white, clear-eyed face.

The banging on the door grew louder.

Peter's face smiled at her from the freezer. "Open the door, Dawn," it said.

THE ENCYCLOPEDIA FOR BOYS

Books were his life. He had been obsessed with them since childhood. He kept lists, imposed quotas, and carefully alternated books of various types to keep him from getting bored. He used to say that every book was an antidote for the last.

And for all this, books could not make him happy. Ralph Holland had been a lonely child and a troubled, brooding adolescent. The first sustained period of happiness in his life had been four wasted years at college, during which he'd opened up and made the first real friends he'd ever had. Coincidentally, he read nothing during this period, not even his textbooks, and ended up leaving college without a degree. He'd learned to be outgoing at the expense of learning anything else at all.

In those first few years afterwards, Ralph held eleven jobs in department stores and factories, each one more frustrating than the last. Once again, he retreated into his world of books. The deeper his gloom, the more he read.

One cold, drizzly October morning, Ralph noticed a "Help Wanted" sign in the window of a Rogers Park used bookstore. He wandered in and within minutes had a job. The owner was tired of running the place and gradually let Ralph's bookish instincts reshape the business in his own way. Within a year Ralph was the manager, and after another year, he had one of the finest rare and used bookstores on the north side of Chicago and three employees to help run the place. Suddenly, books really were his life. His friends, his books, his business were all part of the same harmonious whole.

Through Natalie, his only full-time employee, he met Annie

Stableford, a nurse at Evanston Hospital. They fell in love and Annie moved into Ralph's apartment. It was as though he'd been searching his entire life for the perfect book, the ideal job. Nothing could fill the void, until Annie stepped into his life. And with her arrival, that void receded and weakened, and he began to realize for the very first time that the void was just an illusion.

And then, as quickly as it began, it ended. A weakening of arterial tissue—an aneurysm—had nestled into Annie's brain. Ralph awoke late one Sunday morning to find his arm and leg wrapped around a corpse, her brain a blood-saturated sponge. She was twenty-seven years old.

Once again the void opened, and this time it was no illusion. For days he sat in darkness, unable to concentrate, trying to conjure up all the sensations he'd felt being near her, unable to come to grips with that dry, looming truth: Annie would be no more.

After taking off a full week, he went back to the store on a Wednesday, working with Barry DeJohnette, one of his part-timers. Barry had only been at the store a month and Ralph barely knew him, so their conversation was mercifully formal and trivial. He spent most of the day in his office going over receipts, then ventured up front to deal with the clutter that had accumulated in his absence.

In a corner behind the counter he found a large cardboard box, stained with several generations of water damage. It started falling apart as he lifted it onto the counter. Barry told him an old woman had brought it in Monday night. "She was a sight. And she went nuts when I told her I couldn't give her anything for them. But I couldn't. See for yourself. There isn't a keeper in the bunch." Barry shrugged. "Natalie told me to dump it. I guess I forgot. Sorry."

The box was too far gone to move, so Ralph began transferring the books to another box. They looked as if they'd been dredged from a swamp. There were a few old Time-Life science books, a set of young peoples' classics: *Tom Sawyer*, *Robinson Crusoe* and an abridged version of *Gulliver's Travels*. There was a junior high math book, a U. S. history text, a few magazines too water-warped to identify, and something big at the bottom.

A chill swept through Ralph when he pulled the last book out. Across the top it read *The Encyclopedia for Boys*. The rest of the cover was obliterated by a splattered layer of white paint more than an eighth of an inch thick.

He knew that title, that sea of wrinkled paint. He grabbed the phone with one hand and his wallet with the other. A year ago his mother had given him his brother's phone numbers, begging Ralph to call him. They were twelve years apart and had never really been close; they hadn't spoken in over six years.

"Brian Holland, please." He scratched at the bulbous edge of the paint splatter. "Brian... this is Ralph."

"Ralph! Damn... listen, Ralph, I'm sorry. Ma told me about your friend–"

"No, listen, Brian." He was nervous and talking too loud, unable to catch his breath. "I found something."

"Yeah?"

"Do you remember an old book you had when you were a kid? *The Encyclopedia for Boys*?"

"Aw, Ralph, I had so many—"

"No, no, listen." He took a deep breath. "It had a huge glob of white paint on the cover. Remember?"

Silence... silence... and then, "Yeah... God, I remember that book!" He laughed. "Why, are you going to sell it? I know about your store, Ralph. I mean, if you—"

"No. Listen, Brian. I haven't seen it in years. Ma must have thrown it out or donated it somewhere, I don't know, maybe twenty years ago, probably longer. The point is, someone just brought it into the store."

"The same book."

"The same copy."

"Aw, come on. You're kidding, right? That doesn't...hey. Tell you what. Damn, I can't believe I even remember this. Open it up. On the inside cover, there's that, what...gray and red swirling pattern. And over that, a drawing I did when I was about nine. Is it there? Tell me what it is."

Ralph opened the book to the inside cover, but the pattern

Brian described had been obliterated by brown water stains. Beneath these were faint traces of what might once have been a blue pen line. Ralph held the book near the storefront window, trying to squint the image back to life.

"I don't know. This book is pretty water damaged, but I think... Okay, it's a fish. Wait! I know! A shark!" Suddenly he remembered that drawing from his own childhood, and was able to picture in his mind what had worn off the page. "And a diver, stabbing it with a knife."

They both laughed. Somehow, the tension between them eased, the subject changed. Brian told him about his job with MCI in Atlanta and Ralph told him about the store. They talked about Brian's wife, Louise, their three kids, and finally, in sober, measured tones, about Annie, about Ralph's life with her, and about her death.

And then, death: Father, their sister Andrea.

He didn't look at the book again for three hours, but when he did, he noticed that the stains were fainter than before. The swirling gray and red pattern Brian had described had reappeared, as well as the diver and the gash in the shark's flank. As he stared at the picture, it seemed to pulse gradually into focus. The line-work was studied and precise, not the work of a nine year old boy.

Natalie came in to relieve him at 6:00 P.M. She hadn't seen him since the funeral and was so awkard and hesitant that he had to beg her to relax. She walked Ralph to the back door of the shop, her hand on his shoulder, while he carried the box of books in his arms. Outside he pulled out *The Encyclopedia for Boys* and threw the rest in the dumpster. When he got home he set the book on a shelf in the upper reaches of a living room bookcase and promptly forgot about it.

That night he dreamt that even in death, Annie refused to leave the apartment, refused to let him get out of bed, and clung to him, weeping in terror about the corruption already overtaking her.

Ralph was up late one night, reading and listening to the

all-night jazz show when the phone rang. It was his brother.

"Brian. I was just thinking about you yesterday—"

"Hey, Ralph, I've been thinking about you, too. About... that book. You know, you told me about the damn thing and now I can't stop thinking about it."

Ralph's eyes scanned his bookshelves as he tried to remember what he'd done with it. He saw it, up near the ceiling, lying horizontal atop a row of paperback history books. "Yeah?"

"I was really young when I had that book, Ralph. I don't know... I can remember things about it, pictures it had in it. Things I've never forgotten. Things I dream about."

Ralph crossed the room and pulled down the book. It was warm to the touch and he could find no traces of water damage. He sat with the book in his lap, suddenly realizing that neither of them had spoken for more than a minute.

"Brian? What's wrong?" He heard nervous laughter on the other end. Ralph opened the book and was suddenly flushed with warm air, as though a fevered breath were being exhaled from its pages.

"I want to buy it from you. For some strange reason I'm really curious about that stuff all of a sudden."

Ralph was staring at a crude color illustration, a crowded cross-section of a labyrinthine high-rise in which an assortment of hawk-nosed factory workers, clerks, secretaries, engineers and draftsmen toiled away in various awkward poses. There was something malevolent about the expression on all their faces. Some seemed to glare at him over their shoulders, as though annoyed that he should be trying to deduce the true nature of their activities. He shut the book, realizing they'd done it again. Neither of them were speaking for minutes on end.

"Brian? Is there something about this book that bothers you?"

"No, not really. I haven't thought about it in all these years, but as soon as you mentioned it, it hit me over the head. I mean, a book that was in our family so many years ago, dropping into your lap again like that. I guess Ma just...what? Gave it away, sold it to a store like yours, maybe. I think a lot of things that have always bothered me, things I've never been able to deal with, the places where all my nightmares take place, seem to come from pictures in that book. I don't know... And you're sure it's the same copy?"

Ralph ran his fingers over the wrinkles of paint. "Oh, yeah." He looked at the shark and diver. The ink was vibrant and looked freshly laid. "It's the same copy, all right. Brian? How did you spill that paint on it?"

"I didn't do that. At least, I don't remember doing it. Near as I can remember, it was always there."

Ralph ran his fingertips across the book, noting that the paint felt much colder than the book itself.

"Listen... I've got to go. We'll talk about this later, okay? I haven't decided whether I want to keep or not, but if I don't, I'll just *give* it to you."

He hung up and stared at his hand poised over the book, his fingers hooked over the edge of the cover. Slowly, he opened it and started to scan the pages. He felt relieved by the quaintness and banality of the artwork and the subject matter: articles on test pilots and the newly broken sound barrier, the early days of the Industrial Revolution, the underground railroad, flag charts, dinosaurs, the inspiring boyhoods of presidents past. There was no sign of the cross-sectioned high-rise anywhere.

He stopped on a page that was dominated by an illustration, a deep, murky... familiar field of brown, supposedly a cross-sectioned fossil site. He took a quick inventory of the unlikely arrangement of artifacts suspended in the rock. Pottery, jewelry, tools and weapons of both primitive and vaguely classical design, the bones of animals and... something that stopped him cold.

A vase with a jagged, V-shaped break that revealed a mummified body, its skeletal arms wrapped tight around folded legs and its wide, living eyes staring out of its smiling skull-face.

He remembered those bent, crossed legs -- thin yellow reeds with swollen knees. He remembered the terrible tilt of the head, and the awareness behind those eyes. He had seen it at such a young age, he could remember what his bedroom had looked like when he'd sat staring at the book, and especially this image. He'd dreamt of this figure a thousand times since then, sometimes as an illustration on the wall of a strange corridor from which he could find no escape, and sometimes as a living person, trapped in the dark and buried vase. How many times had he been that contorted figure himself? It was the seed of his most persistent nightmare, one magnified and diversified so thoroughly throughout his subconscious that he was petrified with fear—and yet somehow relieved—to see it in its first, germinal form: a drawing that owed most of its sinister power to the fact that it wasn't drawn very well.

Tomorrow he would be able to dismiss it. Right now he was too shaken to fight off the flood of almost forgotten dream images triggered by this crude drawing. He shut the book, threw it on the floor and went around the apartment, turning on lights.

Everywhere he turned, he saw Annie's things. He hadn't been able to bring himself to put them away. He flirted with the fantasy that the next room he entered, the next corner he turned, would reveal her slender form, her smiling, sympathetic face.

He called her name suddenly, the first time he'd uttered it since her death. He paced from one room to the next, until he stopped in the living room, blind with tears, and found himself staring at the wrinkled spread of white paint on the cover of the book. He kicked it, and *The Encyclopedia for Boys* slid across the rug until it came to rest under a chair. He was aware as never before of how alone he was without Annie, how incapable he was of surviving without her. He had known her for less than two years. And yet, because of her, he was now incapable of living with the loneliness he'd known his entire life.

And then his mind darkened, as he thought about her dead body, now no more than a hotbed of decomposition, a lovingly tailored sacrifice to the gods of entropy. He was afraid, afraid of every space concealed from his view at this moment, afraid to turn off even one of the lights.

Afraid of a shriveled little man, buried alive with his eyes wide, staring out at Ralph with a message.

Two evenings later Elaine, one of his part-timers, called and told Ralph that he needed to get to the store immediately. He hopped in the car and was there in less than five minutes. There he found half a dozen appalled customers, Elaine cowering behind the cash register, while Natalie and her ex-boyfriend, Gordon presided over it all, screaming threats and accusations as they circled the display tables at the front of the store. For a minute Ralph was too dumbstruck to intercede. Then Gordon pulled a hardcover off a shelf and hurled it at Natalie, missing her by a yard but missing one of Ralph's regular customers by less than six inches.

"All right!" Ralph shouted. "Gordon, get the hell out of here until you cool off. Now!"

Gordon smiled. It was not a friendly smile. "This is your fault, you know," Gordon hissed.

"Oh, God!" Natalie cried, "Please don't start on this now!"

He shot her a hateful glare. "Don't worry, bitch."

And with reflexes quicker than Ralph could have imagined possible in quiet, portly Gordon, he punched Ralph in the face and marched out of the store. Everyone else gathered around Ralph, especially Natalie, who cried hysterically over him. Ralph opened his mouth to speak and felt an explosion in his nose.

"What was that all about?" he managed to ask.

Natalie answered, but either because of the punch or her uncontrollable sobbing, he couldn't make out a word of it. She guided him to his office, where he sat the rest of the evening, staunching the flow of blood from his nose and drinking some warm ale he had stashed in a bottom desk drawer. At closing time Elaine left and Natalie came back to sit with Ralph. She stared at him and then the floor, occasionally letting out a pathetic sigh. They sat that way for twenty minutes without exchanging a word.

"Drive you home?" he asked, just to cut through the non-stop ringing in his ears. She nodded.

As soon as they got in his car she asked if she could spend the night on his couch, afraid to be alone, afraid of Gordon. Ralph thought about his own sleepless nights, all the childish dread he'd felt in the days since he'd last looked at the book, and the unsavory feelings about what was now happening to

Annie, feelings he couldn't shake. This was exactly what he needed: someone to keep him company.

They opened a bottle of wine and Natalie tried to explain the circumstances surrounding her and Gordon's breakup. She told him that Gordon had always been very fond of Annie, which came as no great shock to Ralph. But now that she was gone, Gordon seemed to blame Ralph and Natalie for what he could only see as his own—and no one else's—loss. Since Annie's death, Gordon's increasingly indifferent behavior toward Natalie had grown into a vicious neglect.

The wine quieted her and she eventually fell asleep on Ralph's sofa. He sat and looked at her for a few minutes by the single reading light. Once, he even leaned over and delicately brushed a lock of hair from her face. He'd hardly ever seen her with her hair down before. She looked so peaceful in the dim orange light. He finally stretched her out on the couch, covered her with an old quilt, and then just stood over her, watching her sleeping face before turning off the light.

He made her breakfast the next morning and told her a little about *The Encyclopedia for Boys*. She latched onto the subject immediately, talking about books that had left deep, almost mystical impressions on her in childhood but had been lost or misplaced in the passing years.

"You know, there's a book by what's his name...who was he?" She laughed. "Okay, what's that Brothers Quay film...?"

"*Street of Crocodiles*? Oh, wait, I know who you mean. Bruno Schulz."

"Yeah, that's him. He wrote another book, *Sanatorium*... something...oh yeah, *Sanatorium Under the Sign of the Hourglass*, I think it was, where he talks about a book he'd seen when he was real young. It had a huge impact on his imagination. He looked and looked for it later on, but couldn't find it. When he finally did, it turned out to be a mail order catalog or stamp album or something. People are that way about books from their childhoods – especially their early childhoods. And the less they actually remember—as opposed to what they think they remember—the stronger the attachment."

He nodded. "I'd like to read that book. Do you have it?"

"It was Annie's. You probably have it here somewhere."

She cringed. Ralph wondered if something in his expression had darkened at the mention of Annie's name. He smiled. "It's okay to talk about her, you know. Sometimes it hurts more just trying to avoid talking about her." *Say her name.* "About Annie."

Natalie was looking at the floor, her face flushed. She stepped up to him and kissed him lightly on the cheek, and then on the lips. She had gorgeous brown eyes. He'd always known that—he'd just never seen them at work before.

"Ralph..." She took a deep breath, her fingers playing with a button on his shirt. "Maybe you and I should spend a little time together. I just...I mean, maybe it's because I'm afraid of Gordon, maybe it's because of how we both feel about Annie being...gone and all. It's not like I'm rebounding or anything, and I don't mean for you to, either. I just like you Ralph, and right now I seem to hate just about everybody else and I...I just don't want to be alone."

"I don't want to be alone, either." He was struck by how earnest he sounded.

"Don't be afraid of Gordon," she added.

"I'm not. Really. Next time I'll be ready for him." They both laughed, neither sure why the other thought that was funny.

They kept it discreet at first, worried about the reactions of their friends. But the effect Natalie had on him was impossible to disguise. He couldn't keep the idiot grin off his face every time he looked at her, and he seemed incapable of talking about anyone or anything else when she was gone. Every time he saw her she seemed to grow more beautiful. He refused to admit that he could be falling in love with her, but the evidence was overwhelming.

One night, after an evening at the movies, he dropped her off and went back to his apartment. He was thinking about how urgent and tender they were to each other, in every word and in every gesture. It seemed shameful to be so happy so soon after something so horrible, but what could he do? It was overwhelming and undeniable. He found himself trying to conjure up dark thoughts just to appease his guilty conscience.

At his apartment door he heard the phone ringing and scrambled to get to it before it stopped. He fumbled with the keys, but it didn't seem to matter—whoever it was had no intention of hanging up.

"Ralph. It's Brian. Did I get you up?"

"Hey, Brian. No, actually I just walked in. What's up?"

"You talked with Ma lately? I mean, in the last day or two?"

"No. Why? Is something—"

"No, nothing like that. I just called her yesterday, and you know, I had to ask her about *The Encyclopedia for Boys*. You know, the one—"

"Oh, yeah." Ralph's eyes darted to the blackness under the chair. "I know."

"Ma told me the strangest story. She said she got that book for ten cents at an old resale shop on the South Side when I was about three or four. She said I used to look at it all the time. She never bothered to read it, so she had no idea what was in it until years later, when she found it and started looking through it. Well, something about it really got her pissed and she threw it in the trash. She swears she threw that book away three years before you were born!"

"Well, she's gotta be wrong. I remember—"

"Oh, I believe you! Listen, then she told me that one day, when you were five years old or so, she found you reading it. She knew it right away because of the cover. She took it away from you, looked through it to make sure, and then threw it away again."

Ralph was freezing. "So… what didn't she like about it?"

"Well, you know Ma. She said it was full of *lies*. She said it was some kind of sick joke…but Ralph, she claims that those weeks just before she found you with it was when I had my… well, you know about my…little episode, don't you? I kind of flipped out for a couple weeks during senior year of high school. Got in a bunch of fights… I was actually having hallucinations. It wasn't drugs or anything. I was just…I don't know. Going nuts, I guess. The school forced Ma and Dad to send me to a psychiatrist. She says…" He sounded too embarrassed to go on.

"What?"

"She says the day she threw out the book the second time, I just snapped out of it. No relapse. I don't even remember much of it now. I don't think I ever did. The thing is, she swears there was a connection."

"Brian? Ma is seventy-one years old and you know what a… well…" They both laughed. "… a flake she's always been. Why are we even talking about this?"

"Are you going to sell me that book? I don't know if I believe Ma or not, but I've got to look at it. I have to settle this once and for all. I mean, since I first talked to you about this I think about it all the time. I can't even sleep. Have you looked at it much?"

"No." They were both quiet for a long time.

"I guess I'm afraid to."

After their first three weeks, Ralph and Natalie threw a party, inviting all their friends to Ralph's apartment and then trying to be as casual as possible about the new tangle in their relationship. Ralph got extremely drunk and at one point panicked when people started moving furniture around to make a dance floor. He eyed a corner of *The Encyclopedia for Boys* peeking out from beneath a chair. Imagining himself inconspicuous, he walked over and gave it a little kick. Flushed with excitement, he looked around the room. No one had noticed—except Natalie, who watched him from the kitchen doorway, smiling with eyes that seemed to know everything. In his drunkenness he watched the way the kitchen light made the frizzed edges of her hair glow, casting her face into a darkness in which her smile seemed strangely malevolent.

Ralph awoke at eleven the next morning to the faint sounds of music from the living room and the occasional turning of a heavy page. He stumbled to his feet, wincing at the pounding in his head, and groped his way into the living room. Natalie was at the dining room table, drinking coffee and reading *The Encyclopedia for Boys*. She flashed him a cheery, good morning smile.

"This is it, isn't it? The book you were telling me about?"

"Yeah, that's it," he mumbled.

"You know, this is a very strange book," she laughed. "I

mean, look at this section on camping. Read this."

The illustration showed a boy standing alone in a clearing at the edge of a forest, looking out over a frozen lake. Underneath it read:

If you become lost in the woods in wintertime, it is very important to find a way to keep yourself warm. A heavy coat, cap and gloves might not be enough to help you survive the severe winter nights. You'll need to build a fire, and you'll need to do it before the sun goes down. But what if you have no matches? All the kindling in the world won't do you any good if you have nothing with which to light your fire. Many great adventurers as well as spirited boys just like you have solved this problem using an ingenious form of wintertime lens-making.

Find a frozen body of water, as this boy has done, and break away a chunk of ice that will fit into your hands. Hold the ice between your palms and let it melt into the shape of a lens. You can then use it to capture the rays of the sun, concentrating a beam of light on your kindling and starting a fire."

"Jesus Christ!"

"I'm amazed you haven't seen that yet. I'd have thought you'd know this book from cover to cover by now. Okay, now look at this."

It was an assembly diagram for a sheet-metal glider. The book proclaimed:

...it will let you fly like a bird! Try jumping off a small ledge with it several times until you get the hang of it, and before long, you'll be the daredevil of your whole neighborhood!

At the bottom of the page was an illustration of a boy who had just leaped off the top of a water tank and was gliding over railroad tracks, just a few feet above a passing steam engine. At the far right were a group of onlookers and well-wishers, pointing and clapping.

Ralph whistled.

"Can you believe that?" She began paging through it again.

"So you had this very copy of this book when you were little? It's in such good condition, too. Look at this binding."

He examined it. It was in perfect condition, as good as a new book. Better...because there was a warmth to it, an inner heat, like a loaf of bread just pulled from the oven. The only thing that aged it at all was the splatter of paint on the cover.

He had a sudden urge to peel that paint away. He wasn't even sure it was possible.

"You're opening up at noon, right?" he asked gruffly, trying to change the subject.

"Yeah. Coming with me?"

"I'll be along later..." He went to get dressed, thinking he should call Brian, read him some of these insane articles and relieve his brother of some of the uneasiness the damn book was causing him. Or call his mother and hear the history of the book from her.

"Hey Ralph, look at this."

He turned to find Natalie in the bedroom doorway holding the book towards him. Covering an entire page, free of any print, was the cross-sectioned high-rise, broken into over a hundred cubicles, each with its tiny, stern faced workers.

"Is it just me, or is there something wrong with this picture? I mean, besides that the facing page is blank and there's no caption and it doesn't relate to any of the pages surrounding it."

He tried to think of something to say, but looking at the hawk-nosed, wide-eyed faces cramped into those cubicles, he felt paralyzed, cold, as if drawn away from the room...

"So I was wondering, what are all these people supposed to be doing? I mean, look at their faces. The way they hunch over their work and turn back to look at us, as if they're... I don't know... afraid, hiding something. I've been trying to figure this page out for the last half hour."

"What do you mean? Natalie, I wasn't in this room more than a minute before you walked in. Look at the clock."

She did, and froze, turning pale as she dropped the book into his hands.

After she left for the store, Ralph tried to work his way through the hangover by pretending it wasn't there. He made a valiant attempt to finish the cleaning Natalie had started, but within an hour of eating he felt worse than ever. He put on the most uplifting music he could think of—the Ravel String Quartet—collapsed on the couch, and fell asleep.

He awoke an hour later to the sound of rustling pages.

It was *The Encyclopedia for Boys*, its pages flipping back and forth as though by an invisible hand. Ralph edged to the table, a knot tightening in his stomach. At his approach the shuffling stopped and the book slowly settled onto a page with firm deliberation. The binding of the book arched back as the pages darkened and crumbled into a yawning abyss. A gust of warm, humid air hit him, throwing him against the back of the chair.

When he sat upright and looked at the book again, he saw a muddy brown illustration of ancient artifacts suspended in sediment spread out across two facing pages. At the bottom of the illustration, just above the boldface print, was the broken vase and the withered, wide-eyed corpse in his hideous, twisted fetal position. Beneath it read:

BURIED ALIVE

More people are buried alive every year than most boys realize. Immersed in the petty intrigues of their own lives, afraid to deal with death even when it takes their own loved ones, they never question the lifelessness of a rotting corpse. But the residues of awareness defy what we commonly call consciousness. The attributes of the soul defy the dichotomy which seems to separate it from the rich dissolution of the body. Yet there are many who believe that in the thriving ecology of decomposition, human awareness is actually heightened. If there were only a channel through which the thoughts and sensations of those dead could escape into the living world, wouldn't our perceptions—or lack of perceptions—about death be altered? Consider the case of Annie Stableford, pictured above, supposedly dead of a ruptured aneurysm for over two months, but right now, at this very minute, screaming out to you in the heightened perception of her own...

Ralph's eyes moved up to the illustration but the vase had disappeared. A scream tore through the room, drawing his eyes beyond the top of the book and the edge of the table, into the murky catacombs in which he now sat and to the broken vase on the floor before him. Cramped within the vase was a withered female corpse with frightened, crying eyes, struggling to break free.

There was no longer a table, or a book; only the broken vase and the stone on which he sat. As he stood he could hear the rumble of machinery above him, an erratically punctuated drone that grew louder the more he concentrated on it. He approached the struggling corpse with its big blue eyes staring accusingly from within her ancient ceramic prison. She looked as though she had been mummified for thousands of years, but her panic was alive and her voice was Annie's and the name she called out over and over and over was his.

Ralph kneeled before her and put his hand towards the grasping, leathery arms. She grabbed at him, yanking him forward. His head smacked the edge of the jagged V. He pulled away, smearing the blood that leaked from his forehead. She was screaming his name at him and now he was screaming hers back at her. There was a tremendous pounding in the darkness through the arches beyond them, and suddenly, a shrill ringing sound.

He whirled and saw a clean white swelling on the wall. With each ring the swelling pulsed. As he approached it, Annie's cries grew more desperate and the pounding grew louder. By the time he reached it, the wall-swelling had become a telephone. His telephone.

"Hello?"

"Ralph! Thank God! Listen, is he there yet?"

"N-Natalie? How did you find me? Is who here yet?"

"Gordon," she sobbed, gasping for breath, "He was just here. He's crazy! He tore the store apart, and now he's on his way to your apartment. He says...oh, Ralph. Don't let him in!"

He looked around. *Am I in my apartment?* It no longer looked like the catacombs, but didn't look like his apartment either. And the pounding continued. But the screaming was gone, replaced by a voice yelling his name from the other side of the door.

"I...I think he's here now. Look... Call Elaine and Barry and see if you can get either of them to come down to the store. I'll be in... but I don't know when. I guess I'm going to have to talk to Gordon."

"Ralph. Don't let him in. Please. He's out of his mind. He's—"

"Don't worry." He hung up. He was in his dining room, and the book was open on the table. He refused to look at it, but as he passed it on the way to the door he groped for the cover's edge and shut it.

"Damn you, Holland! Open this fucking door or I swear I'll kill you!"

"Be quiet, Gordon."

The pounding stopped. Ralph took a deep breath, opened the door just enough to slip into the hallway, slamming the door shut behind him.

Gordon was almost unrecognizable. He'd shaven his beard, his hair was disheveled, his face contorted into a flushed, hateful smile as he looked Ralph over. "Well, *Mister Holland.* I guess you're wondering what brought me here!" Each word hissed out between grinding teeth.

"What the fuck are you doing here, Gordon?" he yelled. "And while we're at it, what the *fuck* did you to my store? *Huh!?*" This last he screamed into Gordon's face.

Ralph was ready. Gordon threw the same punch he'd thrown a month ago—the same punch he'd probably been throwing his whole life. It was an action Ralph had run through his mind a hundred times since then. It was easy to step aside, move his leg behind both of Gordon's, and throw his arm up and across Gordon's chest, body slamming him to the floor. Ralph was on his feet and waiting just long enough to kick him in the face as Gordon tried to stand. Gordon slumped into the door and something inside Ralph snapped. He pinned Gordon into the baseboards, punched him in the head more than a dozen times, then grabbed his collar, hauled him to his feet, and pinned him against the opposite wall.

"Listen, if I ever see your sorry ass within a quarter of a mile of me ever again, I will fucking kill you dead a thousand times over. I'm not the one who ruined your fucking life, *asshole*. You leave Natalie alone, you leave me alone. Got that?" He let go and Gordon rolled away from him. He staggered down the hall and Ralph followed.

It was too cold to be wearing just a t-shirt but Ralph was afraid to go back to the apartment. Bracing himself against the October wind, he wondered if he'd ever be able to go back. He followed Gordon for two blocks and then gave up, his mind still in the grip of something he wanted to call a hallucination even though he remembered it more vividly than his fight with Gordon. Had he really beaten Gordon up? It was as though someone had just reminded him of something he could barely recall. Every time he tried to picture Gordon's face, a different, far more tortured face replaced it and the surrounding detail began to fill in behind it. Ralph wandered the neighborhood for almost an hour, then he went into the store though the back door, cleaning up in the washroom. His knuckles were swollen and cut, but his face was undamaged...

Except for a gash on his forehead.

When he went up front to get a look at Gordon's handiwork, he found Barry and Elaine cleaning up while Natalie sat listlessly behind the counter. Ralph was the picture of calm command as he consoled Natalie, thanked Barry and Elaine for coming in and promised them overtime. When he told them that Gordon wouldn't be bothering them again, it was with such firm assurance he couldn't help but notice the admiration in their faces.

It was so easy. None of this was really happening.

Ralph finished the cleanup, the gash in his forehead throbbing every time he bent over. Elaine volunteered to relieve Natalie for the rest of the day; Barry agreed to stick around in case there was any more trouble. Natalie nodded quietly the whole time, staring at her feet. Ralph had never seen anyone so humiliated. He walked over and put his arm around her.

"All I did was invite him to the party last night. I thought it would be a decent gesture. He went crazy over the phone, but I didn't think he'd..." She looked at his forehead. "Ralph, what happened?"

He held up his abraded knuckles, trying to draw her attention away from the gash. "I guess I... beat him up."

"You? Beat him up? Oh God, Ralph, I don't think you should have done that. Gordon told me he bought a gun. He says he wants to kill himself. What if he uses it? What if he comes after us?"

He tried to summon up the composure of someone who was convinced this was really happening. So much of him seemed to be trapped back in the warm, dusty gloom of his apartment, snagged in the binding of *The Encyclopedia for Boys.* "You want me to call the cops?" he asked, almost in a daze.

She looked at him with a pained, worried grimace, just now taking in how disoriented he seemed to be. She came over and hugged him, burying her head in his chest. "Oh, Ralph, I can't stand the thought of anything happening to you."

She seemed almost real. He suddenly felt rooted in this place, felt sure this was real, and that the events now receding in his mind really were just hallucinations.

The phone rang.

When it was obvious that neither of them were going to answer, Barry grunted, dropped the broom on the way to the counter and answered it himself. He made a puzzled face as he handed the phone to Ralph.

"Come home to me, Ralph. Please come home now..."

It was the voice of the corpse in the vase. Annie.

Once outside Natalie tried to ask him about the phone call, but he refused to talk about it. He also refused to go back to his apartment, and so they ended up at hers, where he sat and stared at the TV, his hands gripping the armrests of the chair, squeezing them occasionally in response to the inner drama tearing away at him. Thinking it best to leave him alone, she went about her business as though he wasn't there, though she kept an eye on him every minute.

It was almost three hours later when he finally turned to her. "It's the book," he blurted out suddenly. "It...isn't a book at all..."

"What do you mean? What is it if it isn't a book?"

"I don't know. I'm..." He shrugged.

"I saw what you did last night, you know. And I saw how you changed after Wayne moved that chair, the way you went over and kicked the book back underneath it. You looked scared half to death."

"Natalie, was there anything about that book that... didn't seem right to you?"

"Well, yeah. *Nothing* about it seemed right."

"That book did something to me."

"What do you mean 'did something'? Listen, let's go back there right now and get rid of the damned thing."

Ralph tried to weigh all the possibilities as she drove him back to his apartment. Everything around him seemed so unconvincing now, as if the book hadn't triggered a hallucination so much as it had temporarily stripped the veneer from a life that was itself no more than a prolonged hallucination. The dread tightened a notch with every step Ralph took up the stairs and towards the door. As soon as they entered the apartment they heard the throbbing, and saw a light pulsing in the otherwise dark living room. When Ralph turned on the lamp, they saw the book on the table, its cover rising and falling, rising and falling, emitting a white-hot light, throbbing as though it were alive.

"Oh my God, Ralph, it's—"

He let out a bitter laugh of surrender. "You know, at first I thought it was just me... being a little crazy because of Annie. As though maybe I'd unhinged something that had never been hinged too well in the first place. But now I know. It's almost as though it's been searching for me all these years, and once it found me it was able to feed off my curiosity, the attachment I felt towards it, and worst of all, feed off of how miserable I was because of Annie. It regenerated itself from a waterlogged rag into...this...because of me. Because of what was in my mind. This isn't a book at all. It's—"

"Ralph—look at the paint on the cover!"

The white paint was buckling and curling at its edges. Ralph reached down and tugged at it, then gave it a single, powerful yank. The book was rooted to the table, but the paint came off easily in his hand. They never had the chance to make out the image on the cover.

The world exploded around them.

Ralph opened his eyes. He stood inside a cavernous room that was laced with impossibly gigantic cobwebs, carpeted with roaming drifts of dust, and lined with row after row of cluttered, oversized desks. Everything was buried under the fine, gray-brown debris, but Ralph recognized the room, even from the crude representation on a book page, and he recognized the sound of pounding machinery.

"Ralph?"

He turned slowly, sick with apprehension, and saw a figure approaching him from the far side of the room. He stood petrified as the figure gradually focused out of the gloom. It was Natalie.

"Where are we?" she asked, clutching him close to her side.

"I don't know. Maybe we're lying on the floor of my apartment in a coma."

"Your apartment? Right! I remember now. We were..." She turned and looked around her. "Ralph, are we..."

"In the book?" he laughed. "It seems real enough, doesn't it? Nothing has ever seemed this real to me. Not in my whole life."

Somewhere high above—beyond the ceiling, there came a vast but indecipherable commotion, like a faint radio signal at a uselessly high, deafening volume. There was a voice, or at least the tonal qualities that reminded him of a voice... sometimes.

"Ralph? What is that? Is that someone's voice?"

A sudden burst of screams erupted from far above them, and then something that may have been a gunshot. Then, just a moment of silence.

Something stirred in the dust dunes between the desks. Clouds of the stuff began to rise and from within those clouds, gray figures struggled slowly to their knees, as though rising out of an ancient sleep. They all stood, each one of them at least nine feet tall, cleared the dust from the chairs they pulled out from under the desks, then sat.

"Does this look familiar?" he asked her. "Just like one of the rooms in that illustration in the book. And doesn't it all look more finished than it did a minute ago? I mean, there's less dust, more light..."

They walked up one of the aisles, watching as the giants sat motionless, expressionless. As the dust dissolved, the clutter underneath was revealed. Each face they passed seemed more detailed and alive than the last. The faces looked exactly like those in the illustration, with big eyes pulled towards the side of the head, long, sharp noses and tiny slits for mouths. They took no notice of Ralph and Natalie.

Suddenly a mass of thick red fluid splashed on the floor in their path. They both backed down the aisle, and a series of gigantic drops of blood followed their path before veering off across the desktops, raising more dust and splattering the giants. They took no notice.

Ralph and Natalie looked up. High above they saw a tremendous shark swimming through the air. A skin diver swam at its side, cutting a slit across its flank. Torrents of blood poured from the opening, raining around the giants without disturbing them.

The spectacle captivated Ralph and Natalie -- the death throes of the shark and the slow-motion acrobatics of the diver with the blood-soaked knife. There were even bubbles rising from the diver and spreading out across the ceiling.

Ralph had to laugh. Brian would have been so pleased.

But the giants – every one of them -- had discovered Ralph and Natalie. Some even turned their heads as the couple passed. When one of the giants started to rise, its icy glare upon them, the couple ran down the aisle, out of the arched exit and into an immense corridor, its walls a vast field of murals, obscured beneath tendrily blankets of dust.

They ran down what seemed like a mile of corridor without seeing another doorway, then heard a familiar sound, growing louder with each step. A telephone.

Ralph stopped and grabbed a hold of Natalie's arm. "Wait! This is it! Remember when you called me from the store today? It was the telephone. That's what brought me out of this place." They traced the ringing to its source: a small, dark swelling erupting from the wall.

It was an old black rotary phone. Ralph snatched up the receiver and heard his soft, hesitant "hello" thunder across a thousand miles of corridor.

"Ralph? Little Ralphie?" The voice was strained with sobbing, but Ralph recognized it immediately. Brian—not the forty-four year old Brian Holland who lived with his wife and three kids in Georgia, but a hysterical, unbalanced seventeen-year-old kid.

"Brian, you've got to get us out of here! You've got to—"

"Oh, Ralphie," Brian sobbed. His voice was deafening. "God, I don't want to kill you, little brother, I don't want... I don't mean to. I'm being swallowed up, do you hear me? I can't get out of here. You get *me* out of here!"

Ralph suddenly remembered Brian's psychotic episode: Mom and Dad and Andrea all trying to subdue him in his bed while he shrieked and convulsed and raved. Five-year-old Ralph stood in the shadows just beyond the doorway where no one could see him, a big warm book clutched to his chest.

"How long have you been here, Brian?"

The voice was suddenly quiet. "A long time. Maybe forever. Once I was only a scroll. A splatter of pigment peeling off a weathered rock." And he hung up.

Ralph replaced the receiver as Natalie clutched his arm and pointed to the opposite wall, which was beginning to glisten and smolder along a vertical seam. The fissure widened, until it was an arching doorway framed by knotted vines. They stepped through the doorway and headed instinctively towards a dark circular hole in the floor. It was a winding staircase and they were at the top. They peered over the edge. The steps gradually faded into darkness, revealing nothing beyond.

"What if the stairway goes on forever?" she asked. "Or what if we decide we want to come back up here but this stairway doesn't exist anymore?"

He let out a breathless, exhausted laugh. "If it's come to that, it doesn't matter whether we take the stairs or not." He took her hand; reluctantly, they obeyed the lure of the yawning wall and the stairway beyond.

The stairway did not go on forever. It widened and flattened and finally ended as a ramp that eased onto the floor of a wide corridor lined with twenty-foot arched doorways. Clusters of grotesque stone faces with tiny, expressionless mouths and bulbous, hypnotic eyes adorned those arches. Beyond the archways, within ill-lit rooms, giant laborers toiled among brick ovens and over shrouded trays of quivering forms they put into and took out of those ovens. In rooms farther on, other laborers tended gigantic steaming vats in which moaning, slick-tentacled things thundered and splashed. Some of the rooms were empty, black and cold.

From one dark room they heard someone call their names. The cry faded into a tortured gurgling as Ralph and Natalie stopped and peered into the darkness inside. The gurgling and moaning noises came closer and the corridor light began to reveal an animal crawling across the floor.

They backed into the corridor with it following. First they could make out the arms, then the green and blood-blackened rags hanging off a bent and writhing back. It was half of a human body, torn away above the hips, a long spinal tail dragging behind it. It raised a blood-soaked half-face, its single eye glaring accusingly.

"Gordon!" Natalie cried.

"Natalieeee...why'd you..." Gordon coughed, spewing a pool of luminescent green fluid at their feet. He twisted his head towards Ralph, his face not much more than an eye rooted in a skull wound with ribbons of flesh.

"Where am I? I came back to...your apartment... the door was open and I... it was full of smoke...I thought it was a fire... and then I saw...Annie...I followed her and... she... she... I shot her... I think."

He kept his eye on Ralph, and howled through red, grinding fragments of teeth. The pool spread and darkened at their feet. By the time Ralph noticed it, it was a deep, churning channel of water separating them from the raging hemi-Gordon. They shrank away from the green-foamed edges as a figure began to rise within it, a creature that called their names and laughed.

It was Annie, her body shimmering with corruption. She leaped from the water, towering over them, staring down with empty eye sockets.

"I'd have been a lot happier if you could have come alone, *Ralph*. But you had to bring along this bitch, you had to bring the little fat boy there, and you left me to get out of my little grave all by myself."

"Annie? What are you doing here? he shouted. "What does all this have to do with you?"

She laughed, the skin on her face effervescing in a hiss of effluvial steam as the top half of her skull tipped back impossibly before shutting again with a resounding crack!. With a deft gesture she plucked her head off those narrow shoulders and flung it down, shattering it at their feet.

Ralph grabbed blindly for Natalie's hand and pulled her away from the water's edge. As they ran, the corridor ahead was swelling wider and growing darker. Clouds of ash began to spill across the darkness. They kept running, but Natalie gasped for air and grabbed at the back of Ralph's shirt, begging him to stop. When he did she dropped to the floor, sobbing and choking.

"Natalie, get up! The lights are going out!"

"Good! Let them!" There was something wrong with her voice. It was too deep, too old and thick...

He grabbed her upper arms and pulled her to her feet. The bloated, misshapen face wasn't Natalie's, it was Ralph's sister Andrea, who had drowned fifteen years ago. She smiled, her mouth twisting open. The tongue, its spindly fingers clicking against each other, lunged out, tearing at his face before he pushed away and ran blindly through the catacombs, trying to escape the echoes of deep, crackling laughter.

Annie, Natalie. Both of them monsters, apparitions. And Gordon. His brother and sister. Who else will I find here?

He stopped abruptly. Ahead, illuminated by a spotlight, was a large vase. Slowly, he approached and began circling it, searching for the V-shaped crack. The vase turned as he did, always keeping the same side to him. When he finally stopped, it stopped. In the distance, the laughter ceased, and a heavy silence fell. He felt as though the right kind of effort would bring this whole illusion crumbling down around him, but he had no idea what kind of a gesture it required, or where he would find himself once the illusion cleared.

He stood motionless for what seemed like hours, listening for a break in the silence, waiting for something, anything, to happen.

Behind him, a telephone rang.

He turned to see a spotlit phone on the wall. He lifted the receiver. "Ralph, why aren't you happy?" The phone voice was deep and soft, crackling with interference. Ralph didn't answer.

"Ralph? Don't you want to tell me?"

"Who are you?"

"I'm everything around you, Ralph. Everything you've seen and all the things you've yet to see are parts of me. I'm trying to mold a part of myself to please you, but I don't seem to be succeeding. And yet I feel so much stronger because of you. I depend on you, Ralph. Tell me what I should be doing."

"Can I ask you a question?"

"Ask away, Ralph. Would you like to learn how to make a glider?"

"Am I really...somewhere? Is this place real? Or is it all just something you've done to my mind?"

The static crackled louder and louder, then faded off entirely as the voice returned, stronger than ever.

"I don't think I understand the difference, Ralph. Can you explain that to me?"

"Not anymore I can't. Thanks to you."

"I'm just trying to feed off of the things you give to me. It's what I've always done. But when I tap into you, you're horrified at what I make out of it."

"What about Annie? What did she ever have to do with you?"

"Everything I have of Annie's, everything I know about her, is what you've given to me."

He swallowed hard and looked up. There, in the vase under the spotlight, was the corpse, still and silent, as it had first been depicted. Dead for thousands of years...and yet...

"What about Brian?"

"I would love to see Brian again. I can give you a little of what I have of Brian. Would you like that? I imagine he's changed quite a lot by now. I don't think I can change people that way, not without—"

There was a flicker in the corpse's black eye pits.

"NO!" Ralph shouted.

"Ralph, I really like telephones," the voice said, full of embarrassment and admiration. "I can thank you for that."

Suddenly a pounding shook the corridor walls.

"Ralph, don't listen to that! I need to talk to you."

There was a rhythm rising from that slow pounding, one he recognized. He felt an uncontrollable urge to seek out its source.

"Ralph. Listen to me. I am...umm...the wisdom of the ages. I *swear* I am. I've never been a bible, never an epic poem. I'm just a storehouse of simple facts and ideas, an almanac, an encyclopedia for boys. I'm all the simple thoughts of simple people who've given themselves over to me..."

It was a bass drum. Somewhere in the distance he heard the hiss of cymbals.

"Ralph, please listen. You can live forever here. I'm sorry if I've made a few mistakes... failed to understand you... about Gordon. I killed him for you... but there are so many others here—"

"You killed Gordon? For real?"

"I—I think I did. For real? Yes, I think I killed him for real. But for you, Ralph. I could feel you wanting Gordon dead—"

"That's enough!" Ralph slammed the phone into the receiver.

He recognized that rhythm, could hear the song in his mind. Following the sound, he could hear the voice pleading, but as he ran faster and the noise began to congeal into music, the corridor darkened. He couldn't pinpoint a source for the music, even as it grew louder and the floor, ceiling and walls merged into the same darkness and there was no longer anything under his feet...

There was a slamming of book pages and an explosion of light. The song receded behind a wall, a bleed-through from Ralph's next-door neighbor. He looked up to see Natalie, her face smudged with dried blood and fresh tears, standing over the dining room table, *The Encyclopedia for Boys* pinned shut beneath her hands. They stared at each other, their quick breathing falling almost into unison. Beneath the book's title was a glossy field of black.

He looked around the apartment. "Is it over?"

"Ralph."

"I heard the music. I recognized it and followed the sound out—"

"Ralph."

"We've got to burn the damned book. We've got to..." Suddenly he turned to her. "Natalie, do you know what I'm talking about? Did all of this just happen..." Then he remembered the thing he'd thought was Natalie and his sister, Andrea...

"Jesus Christ! Tell me you don't know what I'm talking about." He collapsed onto a chair and looked out the window. It was a bright, sunny day. Of course it was.

She kneeled in front of him. "Listen to me! Remember... Gordon? Remember Annie? I was there, Ralph. For all of it, until we were separated by the channel of water. I ran down the corridor trying to find you, but I kept finding more and more... well... normal looking walls, lower ceilings... narrower hallways. And the spaces began closing in around me—"

"Natalie?"

"—and I stepped out of your closet. When I turned back, the corridors were still there. Then the wall closed up, sealing it off." She began to cry. " But I don't think it's over!"

He pushed her away and rushed into the bedroom. The carpet was soaked a deep red, strewn with the mangled remains of something that had worn a familiar pair of now shredded blue jeans. Gordon's other half.

He peered into the closet. It was the same closet it had always been. And yet...was any of it the same?

Natalie stepped behind him, and put her hand on his shoulder. "Ralph?"

"We've got to destroy it," he gasped.

"Destroy it? Ralph, I think it might be too late for that."

He pushed past her into the living room. The book was gone. "Where is it?" he screamed.

Natalie picked a patch of peeled white paint off the floor.

"Where do you think it is?" she asked in a bitter, mocking tone.

"We've got to find it! We've got to search the apartment! The trash!"

"The store? Why not every used book store in the world? Will it do any good?"

Ralph looked at her. She was terrified, and had been since the moment she'd slammed the book shut. "Natalie... when I... I mean... did I suddenly just appear here? When you shut the book? Or was I already here when you came into the room?"

There was a look of utter horror in her eyes. "You don't want to know." She reached out and took his hand.

The phone rang.

Ralph jumped. "Don't answer it!" he cried.

"Ralph," she said, squeezing his hand, "No matter where we go, phones are going to ring. Sooner or later, we're going to have to answer one."

He nodded. Slowly, he walked over and touched the receiver. It was cold to the touch, but as he lifted it, he felt a breath of warm, ancient air.

FOR THE CURIOSITY OF RATS

I could start by telling you about Monica, the glitter of her skin in the tavern light the first time I ever saw her and the fool I made of myself—trying not even to impress her but just to find enough interesting things to say to justify standing next to her—and the way she took it all in without ever turning her attention away from her friends or the music or all the things that would have been running through her head had I never walked up to her in the first place. Years later, she could still recite my babblings back to me almost verbatim, while I could no longer remember them at all and even at the time she had barely seemed to notice my existence.

Or I could start by telling you about the first time I saw Gretchen, glistening with blood as she burst into the world and began to scream and would not, could not be consoled, in a voice that seemed to know there was no way ever, ever back into that primordial warmth, and who seemed to have discovered with sudden, precise and all-consuming terror the inevitability of death. They laid her on Monica's belly then and Monica cried and Gretchen stopped crying, and I, like an idiot, cried through itching, sleepless eyes, trusting without knowing why that I was a part of all this: I was Father, I was Coach, I was the Y chromosome.

Or I could start instead with a crimson 1991 Ford Tempo. The old man driving it wasn't drunk or asleep or seizuring; he was just a simple, uncoordinated fool who should never have been given a driver's license in the first place.

"It should have been me," was what Monica kept telling me. "It should have been me walking along the curb."

Three years old. At the low end of the growth curve, she was a small three years old. It's impossible to impress on you how brilliant she seemed to me—how ingenious everything that came out of her mouth sounded because of that tiny body, that weightless little voice.

I could start any of a thousand different places, but the truth is... the end is *me*, here and now, walking through this tunnel. The end is beside the point, *nothing*. What matters most, beyond all else, the one place I have to start, the one thing you have to see if any of this is to make sense to you, is the potty chair.

We didn't buy it new—we didn't buy it at all. Our down the hall neighbors Bob and Cathy Grimaldi gave it to us when they moved out of the building. They'd trained both of their sons on it, and from the looks of the chipped varnish and the few wrinkled traces of the decal ornamenting the backboard, they'd inherited it from someone else. I stripped it, stained it mahogany and revarnished it. I did an absolutely wretched job, but still—more than any of the toddler furniture we ever bought Gretchen—it seemed to fit her. The darkness of the wood reflected her own serious manner. She seemed to understand it almost as soon as we set it up for her and, while not committing herself to it, she would sit on it and, by her second birthday, was occasionally making a successful deposit. By her third birthday it was so ingrained a part of her household rituals she no longer even announced she had or was about to use it, merely grabbed a book or magazine, sat herself down and pretended to read.

She had this way of furling her brow with what in an adult might have been called brooding intensity, every time she sat on that chair.

And so, for all the pictures we have of her, taken at weekly or even daily intervals throughout those thirty-nine months, when I first stepped into the bathroom after the service and saw that inch of deep yellow urine in the bowl of the potty chair, the face that imprinted itself into my mind was Gretchen looking troubled and introspective far beyond her years. I turned away, could not bring myself to empty the bowl down the toilet. If I had, none of this would have happened.

The week following the service was a churning, viscous

fluid through which we were forced to move at a constant forward pace. We had no idea where we would be once it was over, only that if we stopped, if we surrendered to despair or exhaustion for even a moment, the churning would push us under, and once underneath we would never be able to pull ourselves up again. I returned to work, Monica was given an extended leave of absence—four weeks—as though those four weeks would make any kind of difference.

I made an arrogant show of pulling myself back together whenever I came home to Monica. She was so much farther gone than I was. She'd been there, she'd felt Gretchen's hand pulled from her own, had seen what could happen to a three-year-old so low on the growth curve, pulled under the wheels of a Ford Tempo. But it didn't matter. I'd held her night after night as she cried, screamed out in anger, quaked and thrashed in pointless god-rage. Now... I wanted to see her *pull herself together.* It wasn't that I demanded to be taken care of, that I feared she was losing grip permanently.... I really don't know what it was, other than to say that I thought—and I realize how stupid this sounds in retrospect—that I could rouse her out of her depths with an inspirational show of pep and enthusiasm.

And so it was that I found myself, twelve days after my daughter was run over by a car, once again standing in the bathroom doorway eyeing the potty chair and its inch of urine, still not emptied, now filling the apartment with an ammonia reek. I winced as I knelt to the seat and slid out the bowl and began to tilt it over the mother toilet bowl.

"What are you doing?" she cried from the doorway. Her voice sounded so alarmed and so different from the brittle wheeze I'd been hearing from her for almost two weeks now.

I gave her a condescending smile and said, "I'm emptying this thing out. I'm cleaning it up and putting it away. What else would I be doing?"

"You can't do that." She would not move, just looked back and forth from my face to the bowl, as though I were holding a gun. "Just... put it back where it belongs."

"Monica," I said with velvety patience, "flushed down the toilet is where it belongs. What's the matter with you?"

"What's the matter with *you?!*" Eyes blazing. "I'll take care of this. *I'll* empty it."

"Fine." I held it out to her, handle first. She looked at the contents of the bowl with an expression that at the time was so puzzling... not quite longing, not quite revulsion, hunger, confusion, sadness, or awe, but a rapid-fire succession of all these and many more.

"Not yet. I'll empty it when I'm ready." I had to take another look at the cloudy yellow pool, as though I were so entranced by her own concentration that I might somehow see what she saw.

Instead, I slid the bowl back into place. The fluid seemed to have condensed so thickly that it no longer even splashed, merely murmured and gulped.

"Do you mind telling me what's going on? Why are we doing this?"

She wouldn't tell me there, in the bathroom, as though it might hear us.

I won't even try to piece together what she told me then. She paced the floor while I sat on the sofa, occasionally looking at the grandfather clock and telling myself, *there's another hour, there's another hour and a half, there's another...* There seemed to be no end to it and yet she couldn't just come right out and admit that... well, what we had here was haunted urine. And yet that was the conclusion she hedged around constantly, always referring to things that had been Gretchen's—the clothes and toys we'd bought for her, the drawings she'd done for us—as though they were devoid of any but the coldest, most anthropological meaning without Gretchen as their common reference point. But by sitting one last time on that little seat and squirting into that bowl, she'd given us a piece of herself (of excess water and toxins her body could no longer use or afford to hold, I wanted to add) and that in a way she had to make me understand, this was really all we had of her, all we would ever have.

Oh, there were so many things I wanted to say, so many cruel and—at the moment, to me at least—extremely clever retorts I could have shot back at her. Half the time I couldn't even hear what she was telling me because I was so busy congratulating myself for not saying anything in return, because I was really coming up with some funny stuff.

Nothing was resolved. I was burning, but I wasn't going to talk about it. I was going to be understanding, something else I was so proud of I was unable to pay attention to what was really going on around me.

So I said, "Just remember if we ever invite anyone over here and they want to know why we have a bowl of evaporating urine in the bathroom, you do the explaining," and let it go at that.

"But it *isn't* evaporating. It *won't.*" I realize now that she wasn't avoiding my point with her reply. She was convinced of her higher agenda, but at that moment I cared about one thing only: attempting to normalize our lives once again, to reduce Gretchen to a somber but palatable memory that we could refer to at artfully poignant intervals. Is this how I saw it at the time? No. It really was Monica I worried about, or at least the Monica that was half of the formula of: Monica Plus Me. I was convinced that I too was grieving in my own way, that there was something noble in my own personal form of grief and that there was truly something Monica could learn from it. I wanted to help her by convincing her to be more like me.

Over the coming weeks I would recall a tenderness that had held us together over those first few days after Gretchen's death. That tenderness had disappeared after the scene over the potty chair, and with every day it remained with us, those bonds between us grew brittler. It did no good to bring it up, I no longer even wanted to know how she'd respond. If I'd confronted her again, if I'd gone to our friends, to her doctor, her parents, how different might it all have turned out? Instead I withdrew, and looking back on it now, it must have been me who withdrew the farthest, so that on the day I came home and found the apartment choking with disinfectant and no trace of the potty chair anywhere and Monica in better spirits than she'd been since before Gretchen's death, I no longer knew how to respond.

A subtle but persistent laughter seemed to lace her every

word, neither forced nor uncontrollable, but to me who at least thought I knew her better than anyone in the world, the sign of something much more than resignation. She seemed genuinely happy. She wanted to be near to me with an urgency that was difficult to adjust to so suddenly. Through those first few hours, I was actually afraid of her. It seemed too fragile to question and yet, after awhile at least, too genuine to ignore. So, without ever casting a light on it, without even making a casual remark about it, by evening's end I just more or less accepted this sudden transformation, and if there was too clear a correlation between it and the disappearance of the potty chair I chose not to examine it.

We made love that night and for the first time, she was the more aggressive, the more talkative and more easily satisfied. Every touch, every whisper, perhaps even each light gust of breeze through the open window only made her reel all the more, and yes, I was afraid, but I am a man and these are things a man wants to believe he is capable of doing to a woman so yes, I was perfectly willing to believe that I was the one responsible for her pleasure.

Now I became the one who was unable to talk about Gretchen, while Monica seemed to cast the girl and the experience in a light that seemed almost poetic. I realized that the example I'd tried to set for Monica, this model of grave and mature recovery, had been a sham. Monica had been a willing victim to every nuance of her suffering until the moment it played itself out and she was able to re-enter the world. I was actually a bit shocked at how quickly she seemed to have put that suffering behind her.

But she was infectious.

One thing we had lost by bringing Gretchen into the picture was the freedom to go out together... spontaneously. Now we went out constantly. Very often, traffic on the north side was so bad that we'd go out to dinner or to a show via the subway, as we had years ago, in the days when we'd never had the money to indulge ourselves the way we were now. Usually, it was Monica's idea. I'd come home or she'd call me at work or she'd wake me up late on a Sunday morning, and announce she'd just ordered tickets to a concert or a play, or she'd announce she wanted to see a movie and how soon could I be ready?

We went to a movie tonight, in fact. It ended less than ninety minutes ago and I can't recall a single thing about it. Halfway through a series of trailers, Monica had to go to the washroom. She made it to the aisle when she turned and called out for me to bring her her purse. Monica has never been one to talk in movie theaters, not even under her breath, not even during the trailers. So it was the act itself, even more than the stress in her voice, that drew my attention to the tense geography here: her in the aisle, me in a center seat, and her purse separated from her not only by my body but the bodies of a half a dozen other people. I looked at her, I looked at the purse, a large crumpled thing next to me, and I looked back at her choking back this horrid curiosity and I motioned silently to her: *don't worry about it... I'll look after it.* She lingered for a moment and then turned and walked slowly up the aisle.

She was probably angry because she'd realized I was embarrassed over her breach of theater etiquette, when in fact there was probably something in her purse she needed or at least wanted while in the washroom. I grabbed the purse and was about to get up and go after her and then thought better: if she really needed it, she'd have insisted on it. And besides, she was probably in there already, and there I'd be, standing like a fool outside the Ladies Room holding a purse. This appears to be one of the key contingencies of my life: when all other deciding factors are equal, avoiding the potential for embarrassment will determine my actions.

I set the purse in the seat and did not take my hand away. It was a soft, plush leather and I liked the way it felt, liked the delicate, fleshlike quality it gave to the contours of the contents within. I poked my fingers along the outside, trying to guess the identity of the underlying shapes. Book, gum, lipstick, contact case, eyedrops, set of jeweler's screwdrivers... and something else, a jarlike *cylinder. Now* what could this be?

Rather than try to guess the nature of this object, I opened the purse and pulled it out and held it up to the screen-light. It was clear plastic with a blue lid, and looked to me like a hospital specimen jar. Inside, darkening, fogging, warping the face of an actor on the screen, was a thick amber-colored fluid, almost viscous as I tilted it.

Monica showed up just as the film was beginning, apologized to everyone she had to step over and then offered me a cute, clipped "Hi!" as she stepped around me and sat, pulling her purse onto her lap. I said something innocuous to her because I refused to behave any other way. Even so, the last thing she said to me before the opening music began was "What's the matter?" I shook my head and smiled. "Nothing."

And then I kissed her, an empty, reassuring kiss on the cheek. I thought of Gretchen, who never tired of kissing me on my cheek, and who had been the main reason I'd shaved every day, even or weekends.

Throughout the movie my thoughts were so conflicting and so deafening that I wondered how anyone in this or any of the five adjoining theaters could possibly pay attention to anything other than me.

Evidently Monica enjoyed the movie. She laughed and gasped on all the right cues and hardly ever fidgeted in her seat. I couldn't even focus on the screen, follow the dialogue or hear the music as anything more than an annoying cacophony. The one thing I kept turning back to, the single image of that whole movie-going experience that I will always remember is the sight of Monica, clutching that soft, plush purse to her stomach, one hand gently caressing an unmistakable contour, her eyes on the screen—and yet not precisely: glassy, far away, so very happy to be here and not so alone as she would have been had she only been here with me. Because there were three of us seated in these two seats: Monica, me, and whatever radiance resulted from the conjunction of her mind and that jar of fluid.

When she finally turned to me it wasn't to smile with recognition or to acknowledge the fact that I was looking at her. I'm sure it was because she could hear me grinding my teeth. She flashed me the what's-the-matter smile, and when I made no response, the smile faded, and she shrugged, returning her attention to the screen, to her purse. To the *third*.

Finally I got up and went to the lobby. I did not go back. I bought a box of Sno caps, sat on one of the lobby benches and attempted to read the coming attractions pamphlet.

"Jeez, did you really hate it that much?" she asked when she plopped down beside me afterwards. She smiled and nudged me with a kind of a hey-snap-out-of-it playfulness. I stood and started to walk away. "Come on," I said coldly. Her gaze was perplexed and hurt, and for an instant I decided to give in, to put my arm around her and tell her, yeah, it was just the movie, nothing more. But by the time we were out on the street, I was back in character.

It was late and the fact that we saw a train pulling away from the subway stop as we descended the stairs meant there wouldn't be another for quite some time. And the fact that it was a Sunday meant it would be a lonely wait. But it would not be a quiet one. My silence during the entire walk was wearing thin.

We were standing by a pillar, and I was staring up at a semicircular arrangement of limestone stalactites on the concrete above us. They looked like tiny fingers.

"Are you going to tell me what's wrong or am I supposed to guess?"

I didn't look at her. "You know what's wrong. You know exactly what I'm thinking."

"Is that right?" She was trying to sound incredulous. *Nice try, Monica.* I could already hear it in her voice. She knew I knew. How long was she going to try and stonewall me?

I did look at her now. "Yes. You do." Our eyes locked and in that silence, we traded confessions, both knowing that once confessed, any break in that silence would be total, terminal.

A roaring filled the tunnel as a train going in the opposite direction pulled into the station. Doors clattered open, maybe people got off the train… I don't know. It was underneath the rumble of that train pulling out of the station that Monica finally said something.

"What?"

"I said, congratulations. Were you looking for anything in particular, or was it just a sudden inspiration? I was wondering when you'd go rummaging through my things and find it. So now you know. What are you going to do?"

"I'm not sure." I paced the platform, moving around behind her, but she did not turn with me. "I should demand that you get rid of it."

"Why?"

"Or at least stop carrying it around in your fucking purse! Don't you realize how—"

"What?! How *disgusting* it is? Let me guess. You think I'm deranged and first thing in the morning you're going to call my doctor, my mother.... Let's see, who else can we call? My friends? Too bad we're not religious. I'm sure a clergyman would have a field day with me. Well... let me tell you how it's going to be. I'm not giving her up."

"Her? *Her!?*"

"Yes, her. I figured you'd think I was crazy. I knew if I sat you down, tried to make you see how it is... how it could be, you'd fly off the handle. You'd refuse to even *try* to understand."

"So you figured it was better to just keep it a secret."

"I figured that if all it was going to get me was an edict *from* you, than it wasn't worth consulting you."

"Not worth consulting me?"

"Vincent... your Gretchen is dead. You stopped being her father the moment that car hit her. But I'm still her mother, and she's still my daughter, and everything we ever had between the two of us until right this moment and every moment for the rest of my life... is ours—mine and hers. And you either accept it or you stay away from us."

I stopped directly in front of her. "How can you talk that way to me? What have I ever done to deserve that? I'm not the one who..." I threw my hands up, exasperated, spun about as though I was going to start pacing again and then turned as though I were going to charge her. She backed away, dangerously close to the platform's edge. "No... wait. Okay." I took a breath. "Let me start over again—"

"Jesus, Vincent. Are you going to get violent with me?"

"No, listen. Please... go ahead. Tell me how it is. Monica... don't talk about me getting away from you. I'll listen. I swear I will."

She lowered her eyes, unzipped her purse and looked inside, unsure whether it was really safe to bring out the jar in this cavernous public place.

"You know what I've always really disliked about you, Vincent? I can't stand this self-congratulatory air of yours, all this *hey, aren't I a great guy, aren't I nice to her, and isn't it modest of me to bring it up as seldom as I do?* If I show you this… if I explain what this means to me, if I tell you why I will never, ever give this up, and you stand there quietly… how do I know you'll really understand me? How do I know that what you're really doing isn't just nodding sympathetically, and all the while telling yourself on the inside that it's really a fine thing for you to be standing here humoring your crazy wife?"

I thought of the night we'd argued whether to empty and put away the potty chair. "Okay. Maybe I deserve that."

"Vincent… if I talk to my daughter, if I spend an hour a day talking to her, if I can feel that she can hear me, if I possess a line that gives me access to her, does it matter if no one else can understand that access? That as long as I know that wherever she is, whatever it must be like for my baby… that I can make her happy by talking to her? Does it? I mean, the gist of everything anybody tells me is: *you're supposed to have been miserable, you're supposed to learn to be philosophical about it and get on with your life.* That's fine… for them… for you. But am I kidding myself if I know that I don't have to be miserable, I don't have to let go, and that it doesn't matter if everybody in the world believes I'm kidding myself or just cracking up?" She pulled the jar out of her purse, holding its base with one hand, the fingers of her other hand glancing the curves *so delicately.*

I couldn't stand it. I tried to step near her as slowly and as unassumingly as I could, but the moment I was within reach, I grabbed the jar. We were both holding it now, but her grip was tight, as desperate as mine. What triggered my reaction? I wasn't even thinking of it at the time, but looking back at it now, I'm sure it was the gentleness of her touch on that plastic, that appalling transference, the delusion. If I struck out at it, surely I could stop it, burst it like a membrane.

"Let go," she hissed, looking around for help, but there war no one else on that platform.

"I won't. Damn you, Monica. I want you back. If Gretchen's gone, *she's gone*. But I'm still here!"

She tried to pull away from me, her expression aghast and then creased with disgust.

"Is that what you want? An ultimatum? If I want to keep you, I have to give up the one last piece I have of my daughter? Is that your masterful solution to all my pain?" She telegraphed her attempt to yank it out of my hands, and in that moment's windup, I yanked it away from her.

"Or is it just your way of taking control of something you have no right to take any control of? Give me that back right now!"

"No." There was a roaring in the distance. Our train.

"You asshole. You spoiled son-of-a-bitch. Hurray! You weren't a totally inept father! Congratulations! You could take care of yourself well enough to survive even though I had a daughter to look after! Jesus, I think you're glad she's gone and the only thing standing in the way of you being really happy is the fact that I've had the gall to grieve for my baby and that having something to remember her by makes me happier than having the privilege of sleeping next to you every night!"

I'd been staring into those strange, milky yellow depths as she spoke. Was there something happening in there? As soon as Monica stopped talking I turned on her again. "Shut up!' You just... shut the fuck up. Is that how I figure into this fantasy world of yours? Something this gives you the stomach to tolerate? Well, thank you so fucking much, Monica! It's been a great seven years, hasn't it?" I was shouting now. Any moment now the light would round that last bend out of the tunnel darkness.

"Give her back to me, you bastard!" She burst into tears. "I hate you!" She lunged at me and I pushed her backwards. She screamed something else to me but I could no longer hear her over the roar of the train. But it didn't take much imagination to read the sentiments on her face.

So much uninhibited loathing could not go without retaliation.

I could feel the train at my back, and I could feel the jar in my hand. What I did not feel was the casual backhanded toss— the jar onto the tracks just as I looked at her calmly, as coldly as I have ever looked at anyone in my entire life. She leaped at the platform's edge, but I grabbed her in my arms as the train roared into the station, only inches away from my back.

And then she screamed—in my face, at the ceiling, at the train—while her limbs fell into a trembling fit, and she turned to that spot where she'd seen the jar disappear onto the tracks. Now there was only the train, the dulling metallic glare, the smeared glass, a dozen tired, indifferent faces behind that glass, their eyes directed towards the hysterical woman and the man clutching her.

"Monica, Monica," I pleaded, but the sound of my voice triggered a shiver of revulsion. She pushed away from me. She pushed once and then went limp in my arms. If I let go, would she be able to stand on her own? Everything was happening so quickly. "I'm sorry. I didn't mean that."

And then came the moaning, soft and unstoppable, as her eyes peeled even wider and yet seemed to see nothing at all.

The train doors creaked open.

"Monica..." I whispered into her ear and then pushed her softly, gently, through the doorway of the train. She didn't look at me until the doors shut between us and I could no longer hear her moaning. She stared at me through the glass the way any woman lost in soul-killing despair would look at a total stranger who just happened to catch her eye.

Except that as the train pulled away, she continued to stare at me and I continued to stare at her until she was out of my range of vision. And then the train was gone. And then, I could no longer even hear it.

I looked down at the tracks. There, by the third rail, was the blue lid to the jar. But there was no sign of the jar itself. And as I looked at that blue lid, a rat appeared, hair wet and matted into a chaos of spikes, sniffing at the lid and the ground around it, as though it were just one more piece of interesting garbage there only to occupy a moment of its curiosity.

"Hey!" I hollered. "Get away from that! *Scat!!*"

It ignored me, but it did not ignore the lid, which it continued to sniff, at one point climbing on top of it, perching as it stared blankly at me.

"Get away!" I screamed. It did not move.

So I jumped off the platform, onto the tracks. Reluctantly, the rat scurried off, in the direction of the next oncoming train. It was late on a Sunday night, and that next train would probably be awhile in coming. So I followed the rat into the tunnel darkness.

And that's the end. Thinking on it now, when that plastic hit the tracks, or the train, it was I who should have disappeared, I who should have been crushed out of existence. Does this make any sense to you? I can't make sense of any other outcome.

And yet... I'm still here. In the darkness of the tunnel, listening for a train, looking for a sign of a tiny rat, or perhaps something else. Gretchen? Part of me knows beyond any doubt that this tunnel will continue to widen, to darken, that the foul odors and trash will diminish and disappear and that I will fade cell by cell into a quiet, gentle oblivion. And yet another part of me knows that I have only one of two options: either I will arrive at the next station and climb onto the platform, or else a train will come before I get there and I will have to stretch myself against the wall to escape its reach.

But the bigger part of me can think of only Monica and Gretchen. Monica homeward bound on a train without me, perhaps so lost she will never know when to get off or what to do once she does. Or perhaps free at last of my smothering demands for attention, for primacy. Gretchen somehow far closer to me now than ever before: these tunnels always smell of urine, and yet now, in the wake of my casual act of destruction, all I can smell is her, the sweetness of her skin, her talc, and especially baby shampoo. It is almost as though every step is just one step closer to hearing her laugh or seeing the glint of her barrette bobbing through the darkness or calling out to me, that word I will never hear myself called again: "Daddy." So I say the word out loud. And then, just once, in a louder, more desperate voice, I call, out her name, just to bask in the luxury of dreaming that there is someone here to respond.

There's that rat again. How at ease the rats are down here, how luxurious the contours of all this rubbish must be, baptized by that last remaining residue of Gretchen's life. I need to confront it, and yet I have no idea what I'm supposed to do once I do confront it. I have *never* had any idea what I'm supposed to do.

Fatherhood is such an incredible sham, isn't it?

Unless it's men like me who dictate the rules, a man can do absolutely nothing for a child that a woman can't do just as well, not to mention all the things that a woman is to her child for which the father has nothing comparable nor even analogous. A father is no more than a lifetime of fatherly acts, and you don't have to look far to see the bleakness, the ugliness and pointlessness of what passes for fatherly acts in this world. And what constitutes a lifetime anyway? *Three years?* I changed quite a few diapers in those three years, and it was I who heard the click of the spoon against that first tooth, who saw Gretchen step away from the chair and take those first independent steps. But what was that? Nothing a babysitter couldn't have witnessed. And yet, I was so proud of myself for being there for those moments. No, that's not quite right—proud that it was me there instead of Monica. Proud that I could claim territorial rights to those moments.

When I was a boy I reveled in destruction, in fire and hammers splintering wood and news footage of dynamited buildings and in fantasies of pounding on the children I did not like. I grew to manhood so proud that I had eliminated or at least suppressed these desires, impulses... these *interests.* I was not a destroyer, I was not a war-wager, a murderer, a wife beater, a child molester, all those myriad things that boys can become. And yet, why be proud of that? Is morality really something to aspire to? In the end, I destroyed Monica, so proud and so insulted and so demanding that it could not possibly occur to me that there was anything horrible in what I did to her, in what I did to the most tangible attachment she still had to Gretchen, all because I found it so distasteful, so embarrassing, such a distraction from what was truly important—ME.

For in the end, I am no different from those monsters who

reduce cities to rubble and the innocent to charred bone, no different from the lesser monsters who've pissed and vomited onto these tracks, dumped their trash and obscured every effort to aspire heavenward that has ever occurred to the human race, reducing it all to nothing more than undifferentiated piles of rubbish whose only lasting purpose is to provide a landscape for the curiosity of rats.

SANCTUARY

The Straggler was suspiciously fat. Moisture clung to him, collecting in sluices within the parallel folds of his flesh. He was already slapping at the Mites that crawled up his legs and shirt when he leaned over, gasping at resistant volumes of humid air, and tried to get the attention of Paul's father.

"He's not listening. He doesn't hear anything."

The Straggler cast Paul a dismissive glare and continued his pitch to the boy's father, conjuring vivid images of the goods in his truck: radios, canned goods, guns, books, personal generators… the list went on and on and seemed to grow longer every time he repeated it. When he gave up it was with a wave of the hand so violent that Paul feared the fat man was actually going to strike his father.

Paul followed the Straggler around the trailer court and tried to see the place through the stranger's eyes. The Crowned Ones wandered in and out of the fog, some not as badly infested as his father, others far worse. The gray-brown hives rose like chimney-clusters from their heads with gaping black holes at the top of the encrusted crowns. The Mites swarmed in and out of those holes, marching along the humans' faces, through their clothes or across their skin.

The Straggler was still wary of the Mites but wasn't as afraid as he had been at first—and probably not as afraid as he should have been. He would shout at the Crowned Ones as he followed them, hover over them as they sat, asking them what they usually used as trading goods. It always ended with a disgusted wave and a shrug, followed by an increasingly bewildered look at his surroundings. Sometimes the Straggler would step too close to the tower-like mounds that grew along the gravel road, then have to leap away, brushing and slapping at the Mites that attacked him. He never seemed to notice that some of those mounds were shaped like human beings, frozen and thickened into poses of erect, skyward-staring submission.

When the fat man finally approached Paul, the boy was scratching his bald, slashed and scabby head and looking at a dead Mite in his bloody hand.

"You! Boy! What the hell kind of place is this, anyway? What's happened down here?"

The Straggler smelled awful, looked awful, and had a hateful sneer on his face. The boy spat into the fog and walked away carelessly, calling over his shoulder, "What's the matter? You haven't seen Mites before?"

"Mites? Is that what they are? What are they doing to all these people?" Now the fat man sounded truly frightened. His palms slid over his face and body, searching out the bugs before they began to dig at him.

And so Paul tried to explain the Mites to him, though everything Paul knew was obvious just from looking at his father for a few minutes: the Mites not only built their mounds up from the ground, but were able to dig into the scalps of higher organisms—dig deep—and build their clustered towers out of the tops of their hosts' heads. Some of these crowns were well over a foot high with bases that swelled in gruesome brick patterns over the hosts' brow ridges. The Mites were everywhere.

"And that's why your scalp is so fucked up?"

Paul shrugged.

"Why don't you leave? I mean, things are bad up there, but you could get away from these things. You'll starve to death down here. That stream you're drinking from is so full of toxins that nothing can live in it. Look," he said, his eyes getting funny and his cheeks started to rumble, "you can leave with me. I got a truck up there." He pointed to the highlands beyond the trailer court.

"You can work for me. You'll eat well, see lots of things. You can grow your hair back. What do you say?"

Paul shrugged again and shook his head. No, he wasn't

going anywhere with the Straggler, and he wouldn't feel safe venturing out of the trailer court with anyone. When he told the Straggler why, the fat man laughed.

"There's no monsters in those hills, kid. No... you know, *real* monsters. And if there were, what would keep them from coming down here for you? Who's gonna protect you here?"

The boy slapped himself in the neck and then extended his palm so the Straggler could see the Mite squashed across his fingers. "They do. The monsters are afraid of them."

"Jesus Christ! Well, I'm leaving and if you want to come along, you'd damn well better tell me now!"

He got no answer, and turned with another dismissive wave and walked away. Paul followed, asking him to bring back some canned goods. But the Straggler wasn't giving away anything and he sure as hell wasn't going to make the walk down from the road again. Paul followed him to the court's entrance, then watched him stumble through the grasses along the jagged shards of concrete that had once been the road leading into the trailer court, oh-so-many impossible years ago.

Within moments, the fat man was swallowed in the rolling fog. Paul stood quietly for a few minutes, listening for the sound of a scream, the starting of an engine, but heard nothing. He decided to see if he could find himself and his father something to eat.

The Beast crawled from a narrow opening in the earth, away from the shrieks and the wet crowded darkness. He stood in the fog and listened.

Not far away, something big and clumsy trudged up a muddy slope. It did not sound like one of the sick ones who lived in the valley. He had caught one of those not long ago, when hunger had driven him nearly mad and rendered him groggy and weak. He had torn it apart searching for meat, but found only shriveled organs, swollen joints, and a heavy, rocklike growth atop its head, which grew deep into the skull, piercing and embracing the jellylike brain. Mites had exploded out of that head so quickly that he wasn't sure whether they had also infiltrated the dry, narrow cavities within the body itself. It didn't matter; there was very little edible meat on the body and the Mites were so voracious that they attacked him immediately, driving him away before he had a chance to take more than a few tentative, dissatisfied bites.

But this one was surrounded by a pungent, alluring odor as it gasped at the thick air and stumbled over the earth. He could feel the vibrations of every step.

He watched as the figure appeared from out of the fog; a human, not too old, and very fat. The human did not see him through the fog, even as he looked around in a kind of cautious confusion. He was searching for something, and was too distracted to notice. The human stumbled off in another direction, up toward the road.

He followed at a safe distance, calculating the strength and edibility of the human, trying to decide whether it would be better to give chase or spring upon him from a hiding place somewhere farther down the path. But as the smell of the human's sweat grew stronger, the Beast grew hungrier, more agitated, then found his legs pumping harder as he zeroed in with silent fury, in a race against time and starvation.

The fat man turned and gaped, face frozen in stupid terror as his belly was slit open with a swift downward slash of claws. The scream melted into a gurgle almost before it left the Straggler's mouth.

He slid his hand through the tear and felt his fingers swim through the tangle of intestines, rupturing the stomach and left lung before gently fondling the beating heart as he lowered the fat man's body into the shivering wormgrasses. He knelt close as the heartbeat quickened and grew erratic under his probing fingers. He looked into bulging brown eyes and let his tongue unroll until its tip ran graceful lines around those eyes, savoring the fear of the dying man, sniffing at the meat as it marinated in the human's panic, before driving the tongue brainward through the eye as his hand crushed the heart within the body cavity.

Wherever Kate traveled, the angelhair followed. It fell through the fog, it fell from the trees in the dead and dying forests, it fell between the hollowed out buildings in the infested urban wastelands that sprawled across the landscape like impenetrable but unavoidable barriers. Once she found herself in a clear, blue-skied flatland of rock, sand, and small, whimpering cactus. Even there the angelhair fell from the sky, marking the path she followed, draping across her shoulders and her thick black hair, sometimes setting a path she then felt compelled to follow. If she stood in someone's doorway begging for a place to hide from the night-cold, there was no way to conceal the thin strands that danced down upon her, and when her host awoke the next morning to find the house smothered in angelhair, Kate was sent on her way. If she slept too long in the open, she would awaken beneath a deep pile of the stuff, hidden from madmen and predators but unable to breathe and barely able to move. She traveled to keep it from accumulating too thickly in one spot, weaving a restless zigzag across the country.

She was moving into the lowlands now. There were things that spread like grasses here, but when she sat or tried to catnap, they seemed not to be grasses at all but vast colonies of worms, waving and wriggling in concert.

Kate followed the path of a narrow, shallow stream that cut through the shrouded landscape. Within it swam small fish, so weakened that it was easy to scoop them from the water. But most of them were bent and crippled by parasites that clung to their sides and slowly sucked their life away. These parasites had thorny carapaces and hooks that dug deep into the flesh. The parasites themselves were inedible and impossible to remove without tearing the fish to pieces. She'd run out of food and would have used her gun to hunt if the few animals she saw were large enough to remain reasonably intact after a shotgun blast. Instead, she scooped at schools of dying fish and hunted for those few—about one in ten—that had not already become a host.

When she first heard the sounds she stopped and tried to form a picture of a creature that would make such sounds. Whatever it was, it was big, and whether it was chewing on the carcass of another animal or just munching away at the worm-grasses, Kate was sure it was dangerous. She moved quietly, scanning the misty countryside. Kate had seen any number of incredible things during her years of wandering, and the more time went on and the more populations everywhere thinned out, the more extreme and unpredictable the life forms became. She followed the chewing and tearing sounds, slowing with every step as they became louder and more focused and she began to imagine in those sounds and scents the presence of flesh, bone, viscera cooling in the afternoon fog.

She moved cautiously and yet was still caught off guard when she came upon the creature sitting at the lip of a great fissure in the earth, neatly tearing apart the body of a heavy-set human male. The creature was larger than a man, maybe eight feet tall if it stood erect, with a body thickened by a studded, convoluted armor except for long, thin legs. Its arms were long, its biceps lined with thorny growths and its triceps covered by the heavy carapace that extended sharply off its shoulders. But it was the creature's head that frightened her most, especially in the moment it turned to look at her. Long and sleek along the cheeks but sharply ridged and crowned along the top, it seemed to have no definite eyes or ears or nose—just a mouth like a long, soft-fleshed proboscis. Without knowing where its eyes might be, Kate knew exactly the moment it looked into her eyes while its lips peeled back to show a ring of sharp teeth. She saw those teeth actually bend into hooks, and in the next instant saw a long tongue dance out between them.

It dropped the body pieces on the ground and roared. The armor on its shoulders rose and fanned outward like the plumage of an iron peacock as it crouched.

Kate raised the shotgun and fired. As she turned to run, she caught sight of the creature's armored wing blades exploding into black, jagged pieces. She ran as fast as she could, her feet directing her to lower ground for speed's sake alone. She could hear and smell the creature closing the distance on her.

She leaped over the trunk of a fallen tree, whirled and fired point-blank at the beast just as it leaped. The recoil knocked her backward as the beast clutched its stomach, howling, and dropped to its knees.

Dazed and winded, Kate wobbled to her feet and watched

the creature thrash upon the ground. It was not weakening; it was not dying. Its thrashing was growing more violent, more energized, and she realized that it was about to rise again. She yanked the shotgun out of the grasping wormgrasses and resumed her downhill flight.

It wasn't long before she once again felt its presence behind her. She could see something down at the bottom of the slope—a roof of some kind—and next to it, a gutted automobile. She tried to sprint toward it, her stride exaggerated and unsteady on the steep incline.

She tripped over a crusty growth and went rolling through the grass. The shotgun bounced on downhill; she glimpsed it disappearing in the fog as she skidded to a stop. Her skin began to itch and burn. Slapping and scratching at her skin, Kate was completely off guard when the creature slammed into her, wrapping her in its sharp, deadly caress.

Four years earlier, Kate had been stabbed in the arm by a woman who could no longer stand having this angelhair-conjuring witch in her home. Two and a half years earlier, she'd been gang raped by a group of Stragglers, one of whom had held a .38 to her cheek as he giggled his way through the act. She knew more about the threat of close-range death—intimate death—than she could even bear to think about. And yet nothing could compare to being wrapped in the thorned arms of this monster, her face only inches from the prehensile teeth that were hooking toward her.

Her ten-inch blade was in her hand. She didn't know if the soft white bulge tucked within the folds of that face was an eye or an ear or what, only that it was vulnerable and within reach. She sank the blade into that bulge just as the creature's tongue-tip sliced open her cheek. It released her and grabbed the ruptured orifice with one hand, thrashing out blindly with the other in a backhanded blow across Kate's face that threw her down the slope. It seemed to take forever to touch ground, but when she did she tumbled out of control over rocks and brittle mounds rising out of the earth.

Two thoughts screamed for attention as she finally rolled to a stop. One, the fiery pain she felt was not something within her but something swarming upon her. Two, there was someone standing above her, a thin and bloodied male. She blacked out while still trying to figure out whether this strange looking person—now kneeling toward her—was a child or an old man.

Paul could see fleeting glimpses of the monster on the high ground above the court as it took a hesitant step downward, then retreated. He had to strain to make out the black shape against the churning fogbank, afraid he might lose sight of it as it crept down the slope to attack. Finally, he caught a brief glimpse of the creature retreating to the high ground.

Paul pulled the woman out of the rubble, struggling to heft her over his shoulder. She was just a little shorter than he was and probably a lot lighter, but she was out cold and almost impossible to lift. He finally managed to get her back to the trailer and stretched out on the concrete at the base of the front steps. His father sat out on the picnic bench, his eyes bulging, empty whites, nodding his head and mumbling replies to the very real voices in his head while Paul examined the woman's face, her arms, legs, ribs. Nothing seemed to be broken, but she was cut badly on her face and hands.

Worse, though, were the Mites. He could see their glittering shells moving in and out of her long, thick hair, moving along her cuts and dancing within the coagulating blood. He ran into the trailer and came out with scissors and wet rags, hastily cleaning the wounds and wiping away as many of the Mites as he could, then began hacking at her hair. Within minutes he had it chopped down to two or three inches, at which point he rested her head in his lap and began picking at individual Mites, crushing them between thumb and forefinger, slapping at those that escaped onto his pants. He moved quickly and with the hopeless determination he'd once used with his father— before the man had succumbed to the sweet, perpetual dream world that the Mites offered and began responding to Paul with violent flailings and screams. By that time it was no longer his father screaming, but the Mites inside of him.

Paul looked at the woman's face as he groomed her. He wondered how old she was. Surely not as old as father. Thirty?

Twenty-five? There was a delicate beauty about her features that no scar or stress line could hide. He had been a little boy the last time he'd seen a real, uninfested woman—probably no more than twelve years old.

He saw a large Mite disappear down the front of her shirt and ripped away the buttons in a panic, trying to grab it before it escaped. Suddenly she was awake, letting out a scream that escalated into a roar. She grabbed his wrists. He tried to stand but her grip was powerful and he found himself fighting to free his wrists and retain his balance as she stood and tried to throw him back to the ground. He twisted his body abruptly, managed to free one arm and break her grip on the other with a downward sweep onto her forearm. She howled with pain, then punched him in the face. He landed tailbone first on the concrete and then squinted up at her, trying to make her out through the thousands of flashing lights that danced before his eyes. When he focused on that face again—that pretty, delicate face—it wore a teeth-clenching grimace of rage. Her hand fumbled at an empty knife sheath.

"I was only trying to get the Mites off you, lady. They're all over you!" He propped himself up on one elbow and pointed toward the stream. "You better go wash yourself off—"

He didn't have to finish. Her attention turned abruptly to the hundreds of tiny creatures crawling over her. She let out a resounding "Shit," then headed off toward the stream. She turned back to him for just a moment as he was standing up. "You lay a hand on me again, mister, and I'll fucking KILL you!"

He watched her retreat and wiped away the blood that was leaking from his nose and into his mouth.

His father moaned and looked at Paul with eyes that for just a moment seemed just a little bit aware and alive. Then it was gone, and his head drooped forward and the eyes went dead-white once again. When Paul stepped forward to push his father's body into a more comfortable position, he noticed several long, white strands of hair lying across his arm and draped over his head. He gathered them together and held them to his face and breathed deep. They smelled sweet and pungent... like the woman bathing in the stream.

They lived in rusted hulls that were scratched and crumpled from some long-forgotten struggle, staring at the outside world through cracked and cobwebbed glass. Had Kate been of a more philosophical mind, she might have taken issue with the idea that they were still human at all. As it was, she could only look upon them with caution and fear, knowing that the only way to avoid their fate was to climb out of this trailer park wasteland and face the thing that had forced her here in the first place.

Which, of course, was the decision all of these people had once made: either risk agony and death at the hands of that thing up there, or fight the inevitable infestation of Mites and spend the rest of their lives in whatever shadow-world the Mites in their heads would take them to. What purpose did these people serve the industrious creatures? What did the humans provide the Mites? They could build a mound four feet tall in a single afternoon, using nothing more than dirt and their own secretions. How were the encrusted cylinders blooming from the heads of these people different?

Paul did not, could not, know. But Paul's father, and all the rest—she counted 24 in all—knew very well. Perhaps that was all they were able to know. It was Kate's overwhelming priority never to find out for herself. She was starving down here, and the few dried rags of meat or canned green beans Paul gave her were not nearly enough. What did the others eat? Did the Mites feed them, sacrifice their own bodies for the nutritional needs of their hosts?

Kate wandered the court during the daylight hours, trying to keep the angelhair from accumulating too heavily in one spot. She tried to talk to the crowned, white-eyed, gently mumbling people who staggered about, trying to grasp something useful in their aimless wandering or in the apparent random building and scurrying of a billion tiny Mites. She tried to keep the Mites off of her own body as she walked the perimeters of the trailer court and looked for signs of the monster in the fog. As she did, the angelhair fell, snagging atop the trailers and on the old rooftop antennas and in the branches of the dead trees until it seemed as though she was weaving a canopy of silky fibers over the entire court.

How many of those creatures—warm-blooded predators, large enough to require frequent meals—could there be in a world where there was very little on which to feed? Surely there couldn't be all that many—maybe this one was a sport, a one-of-the-kind monstrosity. But as she walked the perimeter, weaving the outer edge of her silver canopy, she looked into the fog-laden roads and slopes and could feel their presence, their attention. During those first few days it had been hard to understand how these people could have allowed themselves to be subjected to the Mite infestations; why Paul, tearing himself apart to hold the infestation off a few more precious weeks or months, didn't just take his chances and escape this valley. The longer she stayed, the more she understood. It was the fog and the shadows lurking within it. Once you saw the creature, especially at the range from which she'd seen and felt it, it was impossible not to see suggestions of it in every dark or thin patch in the rolling blanket of cloud.

Kate had to get out. She'd wandered too many years to end up trapped here, scratching her flesh away because of a bunch of gruesomely opportunistic bugs, afraid to leave because she saw hallucinations in the fog that surrounded her. There had to be a way to get free, and as the days passed she grew convinced that somehow the answer lay with Paul.

After their first ugly encounter, she'd kept away from him for a couple of days, always aware of his presence, his curiosity, his obvious and sadly awkward attraction to her. Once she came to believe the reason he'd given for his groping hand on the first day, she let down her guard and allowed him to approach and talk to her. He led her to the most well furnished of the abandoned trailers, he found her scraps of food, and in his own, clumsy fashion, tried to provide her with conversation. Were it not for the horrible scabs and scars festering atop his head, he might have been a fairly attractive young man; his eyes were piercing light blue and there was a warmth and determination in his smile that was almost heartbreaking when she considered how bleak his future was in this rusted, bug-saturated hell.

And so, lying in her trailer at night, sleeping in a bed for the first time in months, she would try to walk herself through her escape, try to rationalize her chances now that she'd lost her shotgun and her blade. With each passing night, Paul would figure more and more into these fantasies, and she began to see reasons why his presence might give her the courage to attempt it, how it was the only way Paul could escape the fate of his father, how his presence could help her odds of surviving.

But Paul was even more afraid of the monsters in the fog than she was. As much as he despised the Mites, he spoke as though he were in debt to them for at least providing a refuge from the creatures in the high ground surrounding the trailer court. And—as far gone as his father might have been— Paul was truly devoted to the man. Kate doubted she could persuade the boy to leave unless his father was brought along.

The solution hit her one morning as she stood in the doorway watching a woman stand unflinching as dozens of Mites skittered over her face and into her towering crown. Kate was already positive it would work when Paul showed up later that day, wiping the moisture away from the shotgun he'd discovered in the wormgrasses no more than twenty feet upland from where he'd first found her.

"Paul," she said, picking a Mite from his shoulder and crushing it between thumb and forefinger, "I know how we can get out of here. You, me, and your father." She reached for his face with two outstretched fingers, as though to pluck away another Mite, but instead ran her palm and fingertips across his cheek. She could feel him shudder. He looked down at the ground.

"Dad too?"

"Yes, Paul. Would you like to hear it?"

He looked up at her. She felt a Mite scurry down the front of her shirt, and saw Paul's eyes follow it bashfully before looking back into her eyes.

"Okay. What's the plan?"

"Paul, a Mite just crawled down my shirt. Could you get it for me? Would you kill it for me?"

The boy swallowed hard and looked away, paralyzed. She pulled him close.

"Paul? Please?"

He lay next to her in bed, listening as she filled out the distances beyond the fogbanks with her tales, her description of the world he'd never dreamed of seeing himself.

"When I was a little girl, I remember blue, cloudless skies... and people. The changes had all begun years before, of course, but they started to come on more powerfully then, like waves of fog just washing over us, killing us and nearly everything else that couldn't hide or adapt. And in their place..." She shrugged and didn't finish, not wanting to scare him too much about the world into which she was about to throw him.

Paul was eager but gentle, awkward but lovingly persistent. As they held each other in the darkness, she whispered a sanitized scenario of escape to him, and he nodded in agreement with every point. She needn't have lied to him. She was sure that this boy, her lover, would have agreed to anything she told him.

They trudged through rolling, hissing clouds of milky white moisture. Kate took the lead, moving quickly while Paul tried to maintain a central position between her and his father, worried that because of Kate's haste and determination he would lose sight of her. He was frightened by the openness, the emptiness of the sloping ground, and of the fog that sometimes hid Kate completely. He couldn't afford to lose her for a second, dependent on her not only for leading the way but for her sensitivity and reaction time to all that lurked beyond his own eyes and ears. Still, he could only move so fast. His father was almost too weak for this uphill climb, and far too awkward to keep from falling on his face every few steps.

"The beast won't dare attack us if it's as afraid of the Mites as you say," she had told him. "Your father will be our shield. Him and his cargo." It had all sounded so convincing. "I know where the Straggler's truck is parked. We'll be able to cover plenty of ground before we have to worry about gasoline." Down there, lying naked against her warm, smooth flesh, there was no way he could not believe her, no way he could refuse.

"Since I've never seen these Mites anywhere else, maybe there's something down in the valley they need in order to survive. We can save your father, bring him back. You can grow back your hair." But the world as it had seemed while she'd stroked between his legs and whispered in his ear was far different from the lonely, desolate plain through which they now climbed, so empty but so loud, so vast and yet—with its clinging, milky vapors—so constricting.

The expression on his father's face was far worse than blank—it was utterly consumed. His head rolled from side to side under the weight of his encrusted crown and wet, gagging songs dripped weakly from his mouth. *He has no idea where we're going. Is there enough left of him to bring back even if the Mites die up here?*

Finally, Kate ssshhhhed them to a halt at the top of a ridge.

"Is the truck near here?" He whispered. Her response was a sharp grab at his cheeks, her palm pressed firmly over his mouth. He shook her away and lifted his father again.

Kate raised the shotgun and squinted into the fog, trying to catch a sign of movement in those fleeting patches of transparent air. Her head turned in response to noises he couldn't make out over the din. "It's nearby. I can hear it. I can... smell it."

"What do we do?" he asked, trying to make his voice as soft as hers.

She turned to him coldly. "We put your father out front. I'll guide him, but he'll walk ahead of us."

Paul balked. "You can't do that. How are you going to keep him on course? Keep him on his feet? How do you know it won't just attack him anyway?"

She pushed Paul away with the barrel of the shotgun.

"Better him than us," was all she said before grabbing the frail man, pushing him forward and nudging him in the back with the gun every few seconds.

The old man seemed to respond to her treatment, falling down less than he had on the lower, steeper ground, but Paul knew it was no use. He watched the tilts of her head, her prods to his father's shoulders to change his direction. She wasn't trying to avoid the beast; she was leading them to it.

He groped for the blade hanging from his belt, measuring how easy it would be to just step forward and stab her in the back. If he killed her, what would he do then? Go on, just the two of them, or take his father back down the hill, back within the sanctuary of the Mites?

But Kate's instincts were less than sure, and when it finally attacked, it was from behind Paul. He smelled it before he heard it, and didn't see the beast until it was almost too late to dodge the side-sweeping blow of its thick, thorn-fringed arm. He let out a scream as he rolled away and couldn't look up until he heard the first shots.

He could barely make out the three weak silhouettes in the fog; the beast—its outline distorted by jagged horns and crests, the woman firing at it and the thin, frail man with the crown of encrusted flesh—on his hands and knees between them, crawling aimlessly, oblivious to it all. The shells seemed to do little more than slow the creature's advance, though it staggered a little more with each impact. It kicked his father away as though the man were no more than a scrap of garbage, then lunged at Kate as she screamed and jumped away.

Paul ran to his father and pulled the dazed man to his feet. His father's eyes fluttered as the pupils spun crazily. A stream of meaningless sounds escaped his mouth on a malodorous cloud. The man had just enough energy left to shake off his son's help and fall back into the wormgrass, sitting with his head slumped forward so that Paul could clearly see the panic of the thousand Mites that scurried about from hole to hole on top of his father's head.

He heard a scream and two more shots.

Paul ran in the direction of the sounds, stopping short when he saw the creature, its back thorns fanning wildly like the wings of a trapped bird, staggering about and finally collapsing on hands and knees as it gave a howl that seemed to fill the countryside.

Paul stepped around the creature carefully, never taking his eyes from it as he approached a winded, wild-eyed Kate. She pointed the gun at him.

"You're not going to shoot me, are you?"

"I can't kill it! I've got to go before it builds up enough strength to come after me—"

"Does that mean I can't come with you?"

"I can't lug around some scabby-headed kid and his bug-farm zombie of a father!"

Paul gazed into the fog; he could no longer hear or even see his father. I'm not going to leave him here like this. He pushed the barrel of the gun aside. "Wait for me a second, will you? Don't leave, okay?"

She nodded reluctantly and he ran back to his father, who raised his head and smiled at Paul, then tipped it backward to expose his throat as he collapsed into the wormgrass. There was blood, but less than Paul would have expected.

They found the Straggler's truck near sunset, but it was useless. The ground around it was dug up in a series of narrow, crisscrossing paths, as though an army of small, vicious animals had passed through, destroying everything in their wake, including the truck's front end. The metal had been torn and chewed, and everything under the hood twisted and broken and thrown out into the grass. When Kate realized that the truck was beyond hope, she threw her shotgun on the ground and began screaming, her fury building until her knuckles left red smears on the scratched white of the truck.

Paul walked around to where the army had torn through the truck's rear doors. Now there was only wreckage, scattered into piles of nearly indistinguishable rubble. There were edible strands and clumps and puddles in there somewhere; the smell of it made his mouth water.

But as he crawled into the back of the truck, the failing light revealed something else. Hanging above him were bleached human bones and dried skin stretched tight over skulls that stared with sunken eye sockets and generous smiles.

As his fingers poked at the papery strands within one of those eye sockets, he thought of the obese Straggler, his hungry eyes and his desperate offer.

Paul jumped from the truck and dipped his fingers into the jagged tear at the top of a crushed can of nectarine wedges. They tasted of metal and mold, but he had no idea what a nectarine was supposed to taste like and had a lifetime's experience with the tastes of mold and metal.

He found Kate, looking dumbfounded into her upturned palm and then staring at the sky.

"What's the matter?" he asked.

"It stopped. The angelhair. It's gone."

"Maybe it... I don't know." He tried to make eye contact with her, show her his attempt at a hopeful smile. "Maybe that's a good sign."

She looked at him, perplexed and unsteady, as though she wasn't quite sure whether or not to be frightened. "I won't know where I'm going. Or where I'm coming from. It always... covered my paths at both ends... following me, leading me—"

Paul looked at his own palm. Hadn't there been a smear of his father's blood there just a short time ago? There was no trace of it now, lost amid the rust and bitter nectarine syrup. He thought of the brittle flesh on the hanging skull he'd touched in the back of the truck. It had been no colder or drier than his own father's cheeks the moment he'd slit the man's throat.

He held out a gray wedge of nectarine and Kate leaned forward, sucking it from between his fingers. She made a sour face as she chewed it and looked at him suspiciously. His own face was calm and cold and unperturbed. There was anger in there somewhere... at her, at his father, at the world; there was fear, too, but it was buried too deep to be much of a problem. *For now.*

They cleaned out the back of the truck and managed to salvage some of the edibles for the next day's trip. He wouldn't let her take down the Straggler's hanging trophies. That night they made love beneath the gently swaying bones and teeth.

The next morning was hot, wet, and milky white.

It had begun as an insignificant pain, an abscess that nagged when he chewed and when he tried exposing or retracting his eyes too quickly; still, nothing that wouldn't go away eventually. It had been the stab wound by the female human that had ruptured the abscess and driven the pain deep into his head and down into his gut, where it still remained. How long had the pain blinded him? How many days and nights had he wandered uselessly, his sense of smell so weakened that he couldn't even sniff his way home?

He'd finally resorted to lying down in the wormgrasses, no longer caring if he was so far down into the valley that the Mites attacked and colonized him. He thought back to the times he'd followed a scent to find it belonged to an animal, alone and apparently uninjured—just lying in the grass, waiting patiently for death.

But the discomfort of his wriggling bed eventually began to overshadow the now diminishing pain. He tossed and turned and finally sat up. He was weak with hunger, and gripped by fear and guilt about the family he'd left behind. He could smell those aching distances and the impenetrable gray in his head cleared into the richly textured daylight fog. He sat for quite some time, admiring the dense hieroglyphic texture of his armored flesh. Then he smelled her.

He stayed close to the trio, eyes focused on the shotgun at her side, the rest of him focused on the smell of her meat and how far that meal might be spread among his cubs. He had withstood the explosions from the shotgun, as painful as they might have been, and he could withstand them again. He would dispatch her quickly this time, cut her and her companions down and not bother to let them marinate in pain and fear before he squeezed their hearts away. He was old, his armor frayed and brittle, and the abscesses were only going to spread and become more obvious with the passage of time. Nothing would ever get close enough to rupture him again.

But this time the shells did hurt and she did not stop firing until he was down and could not stand again. There was a male with her, a young one with even fresher meat on its bones, but he would have neither of them now. They left one behind, however, a rickety old man who barely gave off a scent at all. When he finally stood and approached the man, he realized why. He was dead and infested with Mites. He was inedible... probably. He knelt at the man's side and clawed a neat slit from breastbone to crotch, reaching inside to palm the last glowing moments of warmth from the cooling heart. But the heart was already cold and dry and it seemed as though it had stopped living a long time ago. He held the heart tightly in his hand for a while longer, then ran caressing fingers down the rest of the dried, useless organs, pulling apart the foreign, gelatinous infrastructure that had succeeded them all.

He looked into the dead man's eyes. They were open and staring intently at him. Something inside—the Mites—pulled the cheek flesh away from the mouth, revealing a part of the skull smile beneath. The head rolled for a moment, then collapsed back into the wormgrass.

When he pulled his hand from the man's chest, it was covered in transparent jelly and a thousand scurrying Mites. He howled as he shook them away and wiped his hand across the ground, crushing and smearing the wormgrasses with every swipe.

He was still scratching at the memory of them as he followed the scents home. He had no food and was no longer even sure how long he'd been gone—how long had the cubs gone without food? Had his mate needed to hunt in his absence? But there was a familiar trace floating on the air, and it took him only a moment to remember what it was. The fat man—he'd killed a fat human and prepared it exquisitely. He had been at the entrance to the burrow when the female human had found him the first time. So he'd brought back food after all. The traces were minute—the meat had all been eaten days ago.

But other scents began to intrude on him now. As his eyes examined the violently torn paths through the grasses—as though an army of small, voracious carnivores had passed over this terrain—panic swelled within him, washing away all the hunger and traces of the poison that had flooded his system.

They were the wrong scents. He broke into a run when he caught sight of the black slit in the earth—the entrance to their burrow—but he stopped cold when he saw the tiny spine, curled like a tail and resting half-obscured beneath its shell. There was no meat between the spine and the shell, no blood—just fog and ciliating grasses.

Farther on, another, this one with a few chewed bones

attached, its inedible shell shredded and strung out like a tangled web of wire. He felt something crumble beneath his foot; a tiny skull. And there, at the lip of the burrow, a larger skull, broken into half-a-dozen pieces, its thin, thorned armor spread around it. There were meager strands of meat snaked through the grass. He fell to his knees and pulled the tiny skull toward him, his mournful howl piercing the fog.

He heard a response in the distance. An almost perfect impersonation of his cry. He rose and followed the sound through the fog.

The dead man, dried viscera flopping about the lip of the vertical incision, stumbled toward him, the Mites within working their wonders. The high ground was not killing the Mites at all; it was making them stronger.

The look on the dead man's face was purposeful, threatening when it stepped up to him. It made one last mocking cry. With a swipe of rage, he separated the man's head from his body. The body continued to stagger about, not much less agile than it had been with a head attached.

He went back to the burrow, collected the remains of his family, and placed them in a half-circle around him as he curled into the darkness to sleep, hoping that the diminishing traces of their scents might soften the bleak edges of his dreams.

But he could not sleep right away, only ponder the shape and disposition of this new army of predators sweeping across his terrain and telling himself over and over again ...

I am not the last, I cannot be the last.

About the Author

Jeffrey Osier was born in Chicago Illinois in 1954, on the very day that a CIA covert operation brought down the government of Guatemala. His very first movie theater experience was George Pal's *Tom Thumb*. His very first musical hero was Bernard Herrmann. His first phase of short story writing dealt mainly with the effects of radiation on insects and the awakening of great slumbering dinosaurs. This was followed by a series of stories dealing mainly with the fact that girls didn't like him. This was followed by … oh, what's the use. Listen … he's a dabbler, pure and simple. He plays various musical instruments, sometimes; draws and paints, sometimes; and writes short stories, sometime in the past. He is married to the exceptionally wonderful Cathy VanPatten, has two amazing children, three grandsons, and two cats.

He is currently working on a very important project whose details he is keeping under wraps just in case he never finishes it.

Curious about other Crossroad Press books?
Stop by our site:
http://store.crossroadpress.com
We offer quality writing
in digital, audio, and print formats.

Enter the code FIRSTBOOK
to get 20% off your first order from our store!
Stop by today!

www.ingramcontent.com/pod-product-compliance
Lightning Source LLC
Chambersburg PA
CBHW061248170626
46809CB00007B/2895